PENROD

The O.K. RABIT CO
PENROD SCHOFIELD AND CO
INQUIRE FOR PRICES

"*Eleva-ter!*" *shouted Penrod.* "*Ting-ting.*"

PENROD

BY
BOOTH TARKINGTON

ILLUSTRATED

NEW YORK
CHARLES SCRIBNER'S SONS
1916

To
John, Donald and Booth Jameson
From a Grateful Uncle

CONTENTS

CONTENTS

LIST OF ILLUSTRATIONS

LIST OF ILLUSTRATIONS

PENROD

CHAPTER I

A BOY AND HIS DOG

PENROD sat morosely upon the back fence and gazed with envy at Duke, his wistful dog.

A bitter soul dominated the various curved and angular surfaces known by a careless world as the face of Penrod Schofield. Except in solitude, that face was almost always cryptic and emotionless; for Penrod had come into his twelfth year wearing an expression carefully trained to be inscrutable. Since the world was sure to misunderstand everything, mere defensive instinct prompted him to give

it as little as possible to lay hold upon. Nothing
is more impenetrable than the face of a boy who has
learned this, and Penrod's was habitually as fathom-
less as the depth of his hatred this morning for the
literary activities of Mrs. Lora Rewbush — an almost universally respected fellow citizen, a lady of
charitable and poetic inclinations, and one of his
own mother's most intimate friends.

Mrs. Lora Rewbush had written something which
she called "The Children's Pageant of the Table
Round"; and it was to be performed in public that
very afternoon at the Women's Arts and Guild Hall,
for the benefit of the Coloured Infants' Betterment
Society. And if any flavour of sweetness remained
in the nature of Penrod Schofield after the dismal
trials of the school-week just past, that problematic,
infinitesimal remnant was made pungent acid by
the imminence of his destiny to form a prominent
feature of the spectacle, and to declaim the loathsome
sentiments of a character named upon the program
the Child Sir Lancelot.

After each rehearsal he had plotted escape, and
only ten days earlier there had been a glimmer of
light: Mrs. Lora Rewbush caught a very bad cold,
and it was hoped it might develop into pneumonia;

but she recovered so quickly that not even a rehearsal of the Children's Pageant was postponed. Darkness closed in. Penrod had rather vaguely debated plans for a self-mutilation such as would make his appearance as the Child Sir Lancelot inexpedient on public grounds; it was a heroic and attractive thought, but the results of some extremely sketchy preliminary experiments caused him to abandon it.

There was no escape; and at last his hour was hard upon him. Therefore he brooded on the fence and gazed with envy at his wistful Duke.

The dog's name was undescriptive of his person, which was obviously the result of a singular series of mésalliances. He wore a grizzled moustache and indefinite whiskers; he was small and shabby, and looked like an old postman. Penrod envied Duke because he was sure Duke would never be compelled to be a Child Sir Lancelot. He thought a dog free and unshackled to go or come as the wind listeth. Penrod forgot the life he led Duke.

There was a long soliloquy upon the fence, a plaintive monologue without words: the boy's thoughts were adjectives, but they were expressed by a running film of pictures in his mind's eye, morbidly prophetic of the hideosities before him. Finally he spoke aloud, with such spleen that Duke rose from his haunches and lifted one ear in keen anxiety.

> " 'I hight Sir Lancelot du Lake, the Child,
>   Gentul-hearted, meek, and mild.
>   What though I'm *but* a littul child,
>   Gentul-hearted, meek, and —— ' *Oof!*"

All of this except "oof" was a quotation from the Child Sir Lancelot, as conceived by Mrs. Lora Rewbush. Choking upon it, Penrod slid down from the fence, and with slow and thoughtful steps entered a one-storied wing of the stable, consisting of a single apartment, floored with cement and used as a storeroom for broken bric-à-brac, old paint-buckets, decayed garden-hose, worn-out carpets, dead furniture, and other condemned odds and ends not yet considered hopeless enough to be given away.

In one corner stood a large box, a part of the building itself: it was eight feet high and open at the top, and it had been constructed as a sawdust magazine from which was drawn material for the horse's bed in a stall on the other side of the partition. The big box, so high and towerlike, so commodious, so suggestive, had ceased to fulfil its legitimate function; though, providentially, it had been at least half full of sawdust when the horse died. Two years had gone by since that passing; an interregnum in transportation during which Penrod's father was "thinking" (he explained sometimes) of an automobile. Meanwhile, the gifted and generous sawdust-box had served brilliantly in war and peace: it was Penrod's stronghold.

There was a partially defaced sign upon the front wall of the box; the donjon-keep had known mercantile impulses:

The O. K. RaBiT Co.

PENROD ScHoFiELD AND CO.

iNQuiRE FOR PRicEs

This was a venture of the preceding vacation, and had netted, at one time, an accrued and owed profit of $1.38. Prospects had been brightest on the very eve of cataclysm. The storeroom was locked and guarded, but twenty-seven rabbits and Belgian hares, old and young, had perished here on a single night — through no human agency, but in a foray of cats, the besiegers treacherously tunnelling up through the sawdust from the small aperture which opened into the stall beyond the partition. Commerce has its martyrs.

Penrod climbed upon a barrel, stood on tiptoe, grasped the rim of the box; then, using a knot-hole as a stirrup, threw one leg over the top, drew himself up, and dropped within. Standing upon the packed sawdust, he was just tall enough to see over the top.

Duke had not followed him into the storeroom, but remained near the open doorway in a concave and pessimistic attitude. Penrod felt in a dark corner of the box and laid hands upon a simple apparatus consisting of an old bushel-basket with a few yards of clothes-line tied to each of its handles. He passed the ends of the lines over a big spool, which revolved upon an axle of wire suspended from a beam overhead, and, with the aid of this improvised pulley, lowered the empty basket until it came to rest in an upright position upon the floor of the storeroom at the foot of the sawdust-box.

"Eleva-ter!" shouted Penrod. "Ting-ting!"

Duke, old and intelligently apprehensive, approached slowly, in a semicircular manner, deprecatingly, but with courtesy. He pawed the basket delicately; then, as if that were all his master had expected of him, uttered one bright bark, sat down, and looked up triumphantly. His hypocrisy was shallow: many a horrible quarter of an hour had taught him his duty in this matter.

"El-e-*vay*-ter!" shouted Penrod sternly. "You want me to come down there *to* you?"

Duke looked suddenly haggard. He pawed the basket feebly again and, upon another outburst from on high, prostrated himself flat. Again threatened, he gave a superb impersonation of a worm.

"You get in that el-e-VAY-ter!"

Reckless with despair, Duke jumped into the basket, landing in a dishevelled posture, which he did not alter until he had been drawn up and poured out upon the floor of sawdust within the box. There, shuddering, he lay in doughnut shape and presently slumbered.

It was dark in the box, a condition that might have been remedied by sliding back a small wooden panel on runners, which would have let in ample light from the alley; but Penrod Schofield had more interesting means of illumination. He knelt, and from a former soap-box, in a corner, took a lantern without a chimney, and a large oil-can, the leak in the latter being so nearly imperceptible that its banishment from household use had seemed to Penrod as inexplicable as it was providential.

He shook the lantern near his ear: nothing splashed; there was no sound but a dry clinking. But there was plenty of kerosene in the can; and he filled the lantern, striking a match to illumine the operation. Then he lit the lantern and hung it upon a nail against the wall. The sawdust floor was slightly impregnated with oil, and the open flame quivered in suggestive proximity to the side of the box; however, some rather deep charrings of the plank against which the lantern hung offered evidence that the arrangement was by no means a new one, and indicated at least a possibility of no fatality occurring this time.

Next, Penrod turned up the surface of the sawdust in another corner of the floor, and drew forth a cigar-box in which were half a dozen cigarettes, made of hayseed and thick brown wrapping paper, a lead-pencil, an eraser, and a small note-book, the cover of which was labelled in his own handwriting:

"English Grammar. Penrod Schofield. Room 6, Ward School Nomber Seventh."

The first page of this book was purely academic; but the study of English undefiled terminated with a slight jar at the top of the second: "Nor must an adverb be used to modif—— "

Immediately followed:

"HARoLD RAMoRE∑   'THE RoADAGENT
   OR WiLD LiFE AMoNG THE
            ROCKY MTS."

And the subsequent entries in the book appeared
to have little concern with Room 6, Ward School
Nomber Seventh.

MR WILSON

CHAPTER II

ROMANCE

THE author of "Harold Ramorez," etc., lit one of the hayseed cigarettes, seated himself comfortably, with his back against the wall and his right shoulder just under the lantern, elevated his knees to support the note-book, turned to a blank page, and wrote, slowly and earnestly:

"CHAPITER THE SIXTH"

He took a knife from his pocket, and, broodingly, his eyes upon the inward embryos of vision, sharpened his pencil. After that, he extended a foot and meditatively rubbed Duke's back with the side of his shoe. Creation, with Penrod, did not leap, full-armed, from the brain; but finally he began to produce. He wrote very slowly at first, and then with increasing rapidity; faster and faster, gathering momentum and growing more and more fevered as he sped, till at last the true fire came, without which no lamp of real literature may be made to burn.

Mr. Wilson reched for his gun but our hero had him covred and soon said Well I guess you don't come any of that on me my freind

Well what makes you so sure about it sneered the other bitting his lip so savageley that the blood ran You are nothing but a comon Roadagent any way and I do not propose to be bafled by such, Ramorez laughed at this and kep Mr Wilson covred by his ottomatick

Soon the two men were struggling together in the deathroes but soon Mr Wilson got him bound and gaged his mouth and went away for awhile leavin our hero, it was dark and he writhd at his bonds writhing on the floor wile the rats came out of their holes and bit him and vernim got all over him from the floor of that helish spot but soon he manged to push the gag out of his mouth with the end of his toungeu and got all his bonds off

Soon Mr Wilson came back to tant him with his helpless condition flowed by his gang of detectives and they said Oh look at Ramorez sneering at his plight and tanted him with his helpless condition because Ramorez had put the bonds back sos he would look the same but could throw them off him when he wanted to Just look at him now sneered they. To hear him talk you would thought he was hot stuff and they said Look at him now, him that was going to do so much, Oh I would not like to be in his fix

Soon Harold got mad at this and jumped up with blasing eyes throwin off his bonds like they were air Ha Ha sneered he I guess you better not talk so much next time. Soon there flowed another awful struggle and siezin his ottomatick back from Mr Wilson he shot two of the detectives through the heart Bing Bing went the ottomatick and two more went to meet their Maker   only two detectives left now and so he stabbed one and the scondrel went to meet his Maker for now our hero was fighting for his very life. It was dark in there now for night had falen and a terrible view met the eye Blood was just all over everything and the rats were eatin the dead men.

Soon our hero manged to get his back to the wall for he was fighting for his very life now and shot Mr Wilson through the abodmen Oh said Mr Wilson you —— —— —— (*The dashes are Penrod's.*)

Mr Wilson stagerd back vile oaths soilin his lips for he was in pain Why you —— —— you sneered he I will get you yet —— —— you Harold Ramorez

The remainin scondrel had an ax which he came near our heros head with but missed him and remand stuck in the wall Our heros amumition was exhaused what was he to do, the remanin scondrel would soon get his ax lose so our hero sprung forward and bit him till his teeth met in the flech for now our hero was fighting for his very life   At this the remanin scondrel also cursed and swore vile oaths Oh sneered he —— —— —— you Harold Ramorez what did you bite me for Yes sneered Mr Wilson also and he has shot me in the abodmen too the ——
—— —— ——

Soon they were both cursin and reviln him together Why
you —— —— —— —— —— sneered they what did you want
to injure us for —— you Harold Ramorez you have not got any
sence and you think you are so much but you are no better than
anybody else and you are a —— —— —— —— —— ——

Soon our hero could stand this no longer If you could learn
to act like gentlmen said he I would not do any more to you now
and your low vile exppresions have not got any effect on me only
to injure your own self when you go to meet your Maker Oh I
guess you have had enogh for one day and I think you have
learned a lesson and will not soon atemp to beard Harold Ramorez again so with a tanting laugh he cooly lit a cigarrete and
takin the keys of the cell from Mr Wilson poket went on out

Soon Mr Wilson and the wonded detective manged to bind up
their wonds and got up off the floor —— —— it I will have
that dasstads life now sneered they if we have to swing for it
—— —— —— —— him he shall not eccape us again the low
down —— —— —— —— ——

Chapter seventh

A mule train of heavily laden burros laden with gold from the
mines was to be seen wondering among the highest clifts and
gorgs of the Rocky Mts and a tall man with a long silken mus-
tash and a cartigde belt could be heard cursin vile oaths because
he well knew this was the lair of Harold Ramorez Why ——
—— —— you you —— —— —— —— mules you sneered he
because the poor mules were not able to go any quicker —— you
I will show you Why —— —— —— —— —— —— it sneered
he his oaths growing viler and viler I will whip you —— ——
—— —— —— —— —— you sos you will not be able to
walk for a week —— — — you you mean old —— —— ——
—— —— —— —— —— —— mules you

Scarcly had the vile words left his lips when ——

"*Penrod!*"

It was his mother's voice, calling from the back porch.

Simultaneously, the noon whistles began to blow, far and near; and the romancer in the sawdust-box, summoned prosaically from steep mountain passes above the clouds, paused with stubby pencil halfway from lip to knee. His eyes were shining: there was a rapt sweetness in his gaze. As he wrote, his burden had grown lighter; thoughts of Mrs. Lora Rewbush had almost left him; and in particular as he recounted (even by the chaste dash) the annoyed expressions of Mr. Wilson, the wounded detective, and the silken moustached mule-driver, he had felt mysteriously relieved concerning the Child Sir Lancelot. Altogether he looked a better and a brighter boy.

"Pen-*rod!*"

The rapt look faded slowly. He sighed, but moved not.

"Penrod! We're having lunch early just on your account, so you'll have plenty of time to be dressed for the pageant. Hurry!"

There was silence in Penrod's aerie.

"*Pen*-rod!"

Mrs. Schofield's voice sounded nearer, indicating a threatened approach. Penrod bestirred himself: he blew out the lantern, and shouted plaintively:

"Well, ain't I coming fast's I can?"

"Do hurry," returned the voice, withdrawing; and the kitchen door could be heard to close.

Languidly, Penrod proceeded to set his house in order.

Replacing his manuscript and pencil in the cigar-box, he carefully buried the box in the sawdust, put the lantern and oil-can back in the soap-box, adjusted the elevator for the reception of Duke, and, in no uncertain tone, invited the devoted animal to enter.

Duke stretched himself amiably, affecting not to hear; and when this pretence became so obvious that even a dog could keep it up no longer, sat down in a corner, facing it, his back to his master, and his head perpendicular, nose upward, supported by the convergence of the two walls. This, from a dog, is the last word, the *comble* of the immutable. Penrod commanded, stormed, tried gentleness; persuaded with honeyed words and pictured rewards. Duke's eyes looked backward; otherwise he moved not. Time elapsed. Penrod stooped to flattery, finally to insincere caresses; then, losing patience, spouted sudden threats. Duke remained immovable, frozen fast to his great gesture of implacable despair.

A footstep sounded on the threshold of the store-room.

"Penrod, come down from that box this instant!"

"Ma'am?"

"Are you up in that sawdust-box again?" As Mrs. Schofield had just heard her son's voice issue from the box, and also, as she knew he was there anyhow, her question must have been put for oratorical purposes only. "Because if you are," she continued promptly, "I'm going to ask your papa not to let you play there any —— "

Penrod's forehead, his eyes, the tops of his ears, and most of his hair, became visible to her at the top of the box. "I ain't 'playing!'" he said indignantly.

"Well, what *are* you doing?"

"Just coming down," he replied, in a grieved but patient tone.

"Then why don't you *come?*"

"I got Duke here. I got to get him *down*, haven't I? You don't suppose I want to leave a poor dog in here to starve, do you?"

"Well, hand him down over the side to me. Let me —— "

"I'll get him down all right," said Penrod. "I got him up here, and I guess I can get him down!"

"Well then, *do* it!"

"I will if you'll let me alone. If you'll go on back to the house I promise to be there inside of two minutes. Honest!"

He put extreme urgency into this, and his mother turned toward the house. "If you're not there in two minutes —— "

"I will be!"

After her departure, Penrod expended some finalities of eloquence upon Duke, then disgustedly gathered him up in his arms, dumped him into the basket and, shouting sternly, "All in for the ground floor — step back there, madam — all ready, Jim!" lowered dog and basket to the floor of the storeroom. Duke sprang out in tumultuous relief, and bestowed frantic affection upon his master as the latter slid down from the box.

Penrod dusted himself sketchily, experiencing a sense of satisfaction, dulled by the overhanging afternoon, perhaps, but perceptible: he had the feeling of one who has been true to a cause. The operation of the elevator was unsinful and, save for the shock to Duke's nervous system, it was harmless; but Penrod could not possibly have brought himself to exhibit it in the presence of his mother or any other grown person in the world.   The reasons for secrecy were undefined; at least, Penrod did not define them.

CHAPTER III

THE COSTUME

A FTER lunch his mother and his sister Margaret, a pretty girl of nineteen, dressed him for the sacrifice. They stood him near his mother's bedroom window and did what they would to him.

During the earlier anguishes of the process he was mute, exceeding the pathos of the stricken calf in the shambles; but a student of eyes might have perceived in his soul the premonitory symptoms of a sinister uprising. At a rehearsal (in citizens' clothes) attended by mothers and grown-up sisters, Mrs. Lora Rewbush had announced that she wished the cos-

tuming to be "as medieval and artistic as possible."
Otherwise, and as to details, she said, she would
leave the costumes entirely to the good taste of the
children's parents. Mrs. Schofield and Margaret
were no archæologists, but they knew that their
taste was as good as that of other mothers and
sisters concerned; so with perfect confidence they
had planned and executed a costume for Penrod;
and the only misgiving they felt was connected with
the tractability of the Child Sir Lancelot himself.

Stripped to his underwear, he had been made to
wash himself vehemently; then they began by
shrouding his legs in a pair of silk stockings, once
blue but now mostly whitish. Upon Penrod they
visibly surpassed mere ampleness; but they were
long, and it required only a rather loose imagination
to assume that they were tights.

The upper part of his body was next concealed
from view by a garment so peculiar that its description becomes difficult. In 1886, Mrs. Schofield,
then unmarried, had worn at her "coming-out
party" a dress of vivid salmon silk which had been
remodelled after her marriage to accord with various
epochs of fashion until a final, unskilful campaign
at a dye-house had left it in a condition certain to

attract much attention to the wearer. Mrs. Schofield had considered giving it to Della, the cook; but
had decided not to do so, because you never could
tell how Della was going to take things, and cooks
were scarce.

It may have been the word "medieval" (in Mrs.
Lora Rewbush's rich phrase) which had inspired
the idea for a last and conspicuous usefulness; at all
events, the bodice of that once salmon dress, somewhat modified and moderated, now took a position,
for its farewell appearance in society, upon the back,
breast, and arms of the Child Sir Lancelot.

The area thus costumed ceased at the waist,
leaving a Jaeger-like and unmedieval gap thence to
the tops of the stockings. The inventive genius of
woman triumphantly bridged it, but in a manner
which imposes upon history almost insuperable
delicacies of narration. Penrod's father was an
old-fashioned man: the twentieth century had failed
to shake his faith in red flannel for cold weather; and
it was while Mrs. Schofield was putting away her
husband's winter underwear that she perceived how
hopelessly one of the elder specimens had dwindled;
and simultaneously she received the inspiration
which resulted in a pair of trunks for the Child Sir

Lancelot, and added an earnest bit of colour, as well as a genuine touch of the Middle Ages, to his costume. Reversed, fore to aft, with the greater part of the legs cut off, and strips of silver braid covering the seams, this garment, she felt, was not traceable to its original source.

When it had been placed upon Penrod, the stockings were attached to it by a system of safety-pins, not very perceptible at a distance. Next, after being severely warned against stooping, Penrod got his feet into the slippers he wore to dancing-school — "patent-leather pumps" now decorated with large pink rosettes.

"If I can't stoop," he began, smolderingly, "I'd like to know how'm I goin' to kneel in the pag —— "

"You must *manage!*" This, uttered through pins, was evidently thought to be sufficient.

They fastened some ruching about his slender neck, pinned ribbons at random all over him, and then Margaret thickly powdered his hair.

"Oh, yes, that's all right," she said, replying to a question put by her mother. "They always powdered their hair in Colonial times."

"It doesn't seem right to me — exactly," ob-

"Oh, that's all right," said Margaret. "They always powdered their hair in Colonial times"

jected Mrs. Schofield, gently. "Sir Lancelot must have been ever so long before Colonial times."

"That doesn't matter," Margaret reassured her. "Nobody'll know the difference — Mrs. Lora Rewbush least of all. I don't think she knows a thing about it, though, of course, she does write splendidly and the words of the pageant are just beautiful. Stand still, Penrod!" (The author of "Harold Ramorez" had moved convulsively.) "Besides, powdered hair's always becoming. Look at him. You'd hardly know it was Penrod!"

The pride and admiration with which she pronounced this undeniable truth might have been thought tactless, but Penrod, not analytical, found his spirits somewhat elevated. No mirror was in his range of vision and, though he had submitted to cursory measurements of his person a week earlier, he had no previous acquaintance with the costume. He began to form a not unpleasing mental picture of his appearance, something somewhere between the portraits of George Washington and a vivid memory of Miss Julia Marlowe at a matinée of "Twelfth Night."

He was additionally cheered by a sword which had been borrowed from a neighbour, who was a

Knight of Pythias. Finally there was a mantle, an old golf cape of Margaret's. Fluffy polka-dots of white cotton had been sewed to it generously; also it was ornamented with a large cross of red flannel, suggested by the picture of a Crusader in a newspaper advertisement. The mantle was fastened to Penrod's shoulder (that is, to the shoulder of Mrs. Schofield's ex-bodice) by means of large safety-pins, and arranged to hang down behind him, touching his heels, but obscuring nowise the glory of his façade. Then, at last, he was allowed to step before a mirror.

It was a full-length glass, and the worst immediately happened. It might have been a little less violent, perhaps, if Penrod's expectations had not been so richly and poetically idealized; but as things were, the revolt was volcanic.

Victor Hugo's account of the fight with the devil-fish, in "Toilers of the Sea," encourages a belief that, had Hugo lived and increased in power, he might have been equal to a proper recital of the half hour which followed Penrod's first sight of himself as the Child Sir Lancelot. But Mr. Wilson himself, dastard but eloquent foe of Harold Ramorez, could not have expressed, with all the vile dashes at his command, the sentiments which animated Penrod's bosom when the instantaneous and unalterable conviction descended upon him that he was intended by his loved ones to make a public spectacle of himself in his sister's stockings and part of an old dress of his mother's.

To him these familiar things were not disguised at all; there seemed no possibility that the whole world would not know them at a glance. The stockings were worse than the bodice. He had been assured that these could not be recognized, but, seeing them in the mirror, he was sure that no human eye could fail at first glance to detect the difference between himself and the former purposes of these stockings. Fold, wrinkle, and void shrieked their history with a hundred tongues, invoking earthquake, eclipse, and blue ruin. The frantic youth's final submission was obtained only after a painful telephonic conversation between himself and his father, the latter having been called up and upon, by the exhausted Mrs. Schofield, to subjugate his offspring by wire.

The two ladies made all possible haste, after this, to deliver Penrod into the hands of Mrs. Lora Rewbush; nevertheless, they found opportunity to exchange earnest congratulations upon his not having recognized the humble but serviceable paternal garment now brilliant about the Lancelotish middle. Altogether, they felt that the costume was a success. Penrod looked like nothing ever remotely imagined by Sir Thomas Malory or Alfred Tennyson; — for that matter, he looked like nothing ever before seen on earth; but as Mrs. Schofield and Margaret took their places in the audience at the Women's Arts and Guild Hall, the anxiety they felt concerning Penrod's elocutionary and gesticular powers, so soon to be put to public test, was pleasantly tempered by their satisfaction that, owing to their efforts, his outward appearance would be a credit to the family.

CHAPTER IV

DESPERATION

THE Child Sir Lancelot found himself in a large anteroom behind the stage — a room crowded with excited children, all about equally medieval and artistic. Penrod was less conspicuous than he thought himself, but he was so preoccupied with his own shame, steeling his nerves to meet the first inevitable taunting reference to his sister's stockings, that he failed to perceive there were others present in much of his own unmanned condition. Retiring to a corner, immediately upon his entrance, he managed to unfasten the mantle

at the shoulders, and, drawing it round him, pinned
it again at his throat so that it concealed the rest of
his costume. This permitted a temporary relief,
but increased his horror of the moment when, in
pursuance of the action of the "pageant," the shelter-
ing garment must be cast aside.

Some of the other child knights were also keeping
their mantles close about them. A few of the envied
opulent swung brilliant fabrics from their shoulders
airily, showing off hired splendours from a professional costumer's stock, while one or two were insult-
ing examples of parental indulgence, particularly little
Maurice Levy, the Child Sir Galahad. This shrink-
ing person went clamourously about, making it known
everywhere that the best tailor in town had been
dazzled by a great sum into constructing his costume.
It consisted of blue velvet knickerbockers, a white
satin waistcoat, and a beautifully cut little swallow-
tailed coat with pearl buttons. The medieval and
artistic triumph was completed by a mantle of yellow
velvet, and little white boots, sporting gold tassels.

All this radiance paused in a brilliant career and
addressed the Child Sir Lancelot, gathering an immediately formed semicircular audience of little girls.
Woman was ever the trailer of magnificence.

"What *you* got on?" inquired Mr. Levy, after dis-
pensing information. "What you got on under that
ole golf cape?"

Penrod looked upon him coldly. At other times
his questioner would have approached him with deference, even with apprehension. But to-day the
Child Sir Galahad was somewhat intoxicated with
the power of his own beauty.

"What *you* got on?" he repeated.

"Oh, nothin'," said Penrod, with an indifference
assumed at great cost to his nervous system.

The elate Maurice was inspired to set up as a
wit. "Then you're nakid!" he shouted exultantly.
"Penrod Schofield says he hasn't got nothin' on
under that ole golf cape! He's nakid! He's nakid!"

The indelicate little girls giggled delightedly, and
a javelin pierced the inwards of Penrod when he saw
that the Child Elaine, amber-curled and beautiful
Marjorie Jones, lifted golden laughter to the horrid
jest.

Other boys and girls came flocking to the up-
roar. "He's nakid, he's nakid!" shrieked the
Child Sir Galahad. "Penrod Schofield's nakid!
He's *na-a-a-kid!*"

"Hush, hush!" said Mrs. Lora Rewbush, pushing

her way into the group. "Remember, we are all little knights and ladies to-day. Little knights and ladies of the Table Round would not make so much noise. Now children, we must begin to take our places on the stage. Is everybody here?"

Penrod made his escape under cover of this diversion: he slid behind Mrs. Lora Rewbush, and being near a door, opened it unnoticed and went out quickly, closing it behind him. He found himself in a narrow and vacant hallway which led to a door marked "Janitor's Room."

Burning with outrage, heart-sick at the sweet, cold-blooded laughter of Marjorie Jones, Penrod rested his elbows upon a window-sill and speculated upon the effects of a leap from the second story. One of the reasons he gave it up was his desire to live on Maurice Levy's account: already he was forming educational plans for the Child Sir Galahad.

A stout man in blue overalls passed through the hallway muttering to himself petulantly. "I reckon they'll find that hall hot enough *now!*" he said, conveying to Penrod an impression that some too feminine women had sent him upon an unreasonable errand to the furnace. He went into the Janitor's Room and, emerging a moment later, minus the overalls, passed Penrod again with a bass rumble — "Dern 'em!" it seemed he said — and made a gloomy exit by the door at the upper end of the hallway.

The conglomerate and delicate rustle of a large, mannerly audience was heard as the janitor opened and closed the door; and stage-fright seized the boy. The orchestra began an overture, and, at that, Penrod, trembling violently, tiptoed down the hall into the Janitor's Room. It was a cul-de-sac: there was no outlet save by the way he had come.

Despairingly he doffed his mantle and looked down upon himself for a last sickening assurance that the stockings were as obviously and disgracefully Margaret's as they had seemed in the mirror at home. For a moment he was encouraged: perhaps he was no worse than some of the other boys. Then he noticed that a safety-pin had opened; one of those connecting the stockings with his trunks. He sat down to fasten it and his eye fell for the first time with particular attention upon the trunks. Until this instant he had been preoccupied with the stockings.

Slowly recognition dawned in his eyes.

The Schofields' house stood on a corner at the intersection of two main-travelled streets; the fence was low, and the publicity obtained by the washable

portion of the family apparel, on Mondays, had
often been painful to Penrod; for boys have a peculiar sensitiveness in these matters. A plain, matter-
of-fact washerwoman, employed by Mrs. Schofield,
never left anything to the imagination of the passer-
by; and of all her calm display the scarlet flaunting
of his father's winter wear had most abashed Penrod. One day Marjorie Jones, all gold and starch,
had passed when the dreadful things were on the
line: Penrod had hidden himself, shuddering. The
whole town, he was convinced, knew these garments
intimately and derisively.

And now, as he sat in the janitor's chair, the horrible and paralyzing recognition came. He had not
an instant's doubt that every fellow actor, as well as
every soul in the audience, would recognize what his
mother and sister had put upon him. For as the
awful truth became plain to himself it seemed bla-
zoned to the world; and far, far louder than the
stockings, the trunks did fairly bellow the grisly
secret: *whose* they were and WHAT they were!

Most people have suffered in a dream the experience of finding themselves very inadequately clad
in the midst of a crowd of well-dressed people, and
such dreamers' sensations are comparable to Pen-

rod's, though faintly, because Penrod was awake and in much too full possession of the most active capacities for anguish.

A human male whose dress has been damaged, or reveals some vital lack, suffers from a hideous and shameful loneliness which makes every second absolutely unbearable until he is again as others of his sex and species; and there is no act or sin whatever, too desperate for him in his struggle to attain that condition. Also, there is absolutely no embarrassment possible to a woman which is comparable to that of a man under corresponding circumstances; and in this a boy is a man. Gazing upon the ghastly trunks, the stricken Penrod felt that he was a degree worse than nude; and a great horror of himself filled his soul.

"Penrod Schofield!"

The door into the hallway opened, and a voice demanded him. He could not be seen from the hallway, but the hue and the cry was up; and he knew he must be taken. It was only a question of seconds. He huddled in his chair.

"Penrod Schofield!" cried Mrs. Lora Rewbush angrily.

The distracted boy rose and, as he did so, a long

pin sank deep into his back. He extracted it frenziedly, which brought to his ears a protracted and sonorous ripping, too easily located by a final gesture of horror.

"Penrod Schofield!" Mrs. Lora Rewbush had come out into the hallway.

And now, in this extremity, when all seemed lost indeed, particularly including honour, the dilating eye of the outlaw fell upon the blue overalls which the janitor had left hanging upon a peg.

Inspiration and action were almost simultaneous.

CHAPTER V

THE PAGEANT OF THE TABLE ROUND

PENROD!" Mrs. Lora Rewbush stood in the doorway, indignantly gazing upon a Child Sir Lancelot mantled to the heels. "Do you know that you have kept an audience of five hundred people waiting for ten minutes?" She, also, detained the five hundred while she spake further.

"Well," said Penrod contentedly, as he followed her toward the buzzing stage, "I was just sitting there thinking."

Two minutes later the curtain rose on a medieval castle hall richly done in the new stage-craft made in Germany and consisting of pink and blue cheese-cloth. The Child King Arthur and the Child Queen Guinevere were disclosed upon thrones, with the Child Elaine and many other celebrities in attendance; while about fifteen Child Knights were seated at a dining-room table round, which was covered with a large Oriental rug, and displayed (for the knights' refreshment) a banquet service of silver loving-cups and trophies, borrowed from the Country Club and some local automobile manufacturers.

In addition to this splendour, potted plants and palms have seldom been more lavishly used in any castle on the stage or off. The footlights were aided by a "spot-light" from the rear of the hall; and the children were revealed in a blaze of glory.

A hushed, multitudinous "*O-oh*" of admiration came from the decorous and delighted audience. Then the children sang feebly:

> "Chuldrun of the Tabul Round,
>   Lit-tul knights and ladies we.
>   Let our voy-siz all resound
>   Faith and hope and charitee!"

The Child King Arthur rose, extended his scep-

tre with the decisive gesture of a semaphore, and
spake:

> "Each littul knight and lady born
>   Has noble deeds *to* perform
>   In *thee* child-world of shivullree,
>   No matter how small his share may be.
>   Let each advance and tell in turn
>   What claim has each to knighthood earn."

The Child Sir Mordred, the villain of this piece,
rose in his place at the table round, and piped the
only lines ever written by Mrs. Lora Rewbush which
Penrod Schofield could have pronounced without
loathing. Georgie Bassett, a really angelic boy, had
been selected for the rôle of Mordred. His perfect
conduct had earned for him the sardonic sobriquet,
"The Little Gentleman," among his boy acquaintances. (Naturally he had no friends.) Hence the
other boys supposed that he had been selected for
the wicked Mordred as a reward of virtue. He declaimed serenely:

> "I hight Sir Mordred the Child, and I teach
>   Lessons of selfishest evil, and reach
>   Out into darkness. Thoughtless, unkind,
>   And ruthless is Mordred, and unrefined."

The Child Mordred was properly rebuked and
denied the accolade, though, like the others, he
seemed to have assumed the title already.   He made
a plotter's exit.   Whereupon Maurice Levy rose,
bowed, announced that he highted the Child Sir
Galahad, and continued with perfect *sang-froid:*

> "I am the purest of the pure.
>   I have but kindest thoughts each day.
> I give my riches to the poor,
>   And follow in the Master's way."

This elicited tokens of approval from the Child
King Arthur, and he bade Maurice "stand forth"
and come near the throne, a command obeyed with
the easy grace of conscious merit.

It was Penrod's turn.   He stepped back from his
chair, the table between him and the audience, and
began in a high, breathless monotone:

> "I hight Sir Lancelot du Lake, the Child,
>   Gentul-hearted, meek, and mild.
>   What though I'm *but* a littul child,
>   Gentul-heartud, meek, and mild,
>   I do my share though but — though but —— "

Penrod paused and gulped.   The voice of Mrs.

Lora Rewbush was heard from the wings, prompting irritably, and the Child Sir Lancelot repeated:

"I do my share though but — though but a tot.
I pray you knight Sir Lancelot!"

This also met the royal favour, and Penrod was bidden to join Sir Galahad at the throne. As he crossed the stage, Mrs. Schofield whispered to Margaret:

"That boy! He's unpinned his mantle and fixed it to cover his whole costume. After we worked so hard to make it becoming!"

"Never mind; he'll have to take the cape off in a minute," returned Margaret. She leaned forward suddenly, narrowing her eyes to see better. "What *is* that thing hanging about his left ankle?" she whispered uneasily. "How queer! He must have got tangled in something."

"Where?" asked Mrs. Schofield, in alarm.

"His left foot. It makes him stumble. Don't you see? It looks — it looks like an elephant's foot!"

The Child Sir Lancelot and the Child Sir Galahad clasped hands before their Child King. Penrod was conscious of a great uplift; in a moment he would

have to throw aside his mantle, but even so he was
protected and sheltered in the human garment of a
man. His stage-fright had passed, for the audience
was but an indistinguishable blur of darkness beyond the dazzling lights. His most repulsive speech
(that in which he proclaimed himself a "tot") was
over and done with; and now at last the small, moist
hand of the Child Sir Galahad lay within his own.
Craftily his brown fingers stole from Maurice's
palm to the wrist. The two boys declaimed in
concert:

"We are two chuldrun of the Tabul Round
    Strewing kindness all a-round.
With love and good deeds striving ever for the best,
    May our littul efforts e'er be blest.
Two littul hearts we offer.   See
United in love, faith, hope, and char —*Ow!*"

The conclusion of the duet was marred. The
Child Sir Galahad suddenly stiffened, and, uttering
an irrepressible shriek of anguish, gave a brief exhibition of the contortionist's art. (*"He's twistin'
my wrist!   Dern you, leggo!"*)

The voice of Mrs. Lora Rewbush was again heard
from the wings; it sounded bloodthirsty. Penrod
released his victim; and the Child King Arthur,

somewhat disconcerted, extended his sceptre and, with the assistance of the enraged prompter, said:

> " Sweet child-friends of the Tabul Round,
>   In brotherly love and kindness abound,
>   Sir Lancelot, you have spoken well,
>   Sir Galahad, too, as clear as bell.
>   So now pray doff your mantles gay.
>   You shall be knighted this very day."

And Penrod doffed his mantle.

Simultaneously, a thick and vasty gasp came from the audience, as from five hundred bathers in a wholly unexpected surf. This gasp was punctuated irregularly, over the auditorium, by imperfectly subdued screams both of dismay and incredulous joy, and by two dismal shrieks. Altogether it was an extraordinary sound, a sound never to be forgotten by any one who heard it. It was almost as unforgettable as the sight which caused it; the word "sight" being here used in its vernacular sense, for Penrod, standing unmantled and revealed in all the medieval and artistic glory of the janitor's blue overalls, falls within its meaning.

The janitor was a heavy man, and his overalls, upon Penrod, were merely oceanic. The boy was at once swaddled and lost within their blue gulfs and vast saggings; and the left leg, too hastily rolled up, had descended with a distinctively elephantine effect, as Margaret had observed. Certainly, the Child Sir Lancelot was at least a sight.

It is probable that a great many in that hall must have had, even then, a consciousness that they were looking on at History in the Making. A supreme act is recognizable at sight: it bears the birthmark of immortality. But Penrod, that marvellous boy, had begun to declaim, even with the gesture of flinging off his mantle for the accolade:

> "I first, the Child Sir Lancelot du Lake,
>   Will volunteer to knighthood take,
>   And kneeling here before your throne
>   I vow to ——"

He finished his speech unheard. The audience had recovered breath, but had lost self-control, and there ensued something later described by a participant as a sort of cultured riot.

The actors in the "pageant" were not so dumfounded by Penrod's costume as might have been expected. A few precocious geniuses perceived that the overalls were the Child Lancelot's own comment on maternal intentions; and these were profoundly impressed: they regarded him with the grisly admiration of young and ambitious criminals for a jailmate about to be distinguished by hanging. But most of the children simply took it to be the case (a little strange, but not startling) that Penrod's mother had dressed him like that — which is pathetic. They tried to go on with the "pageant."

They made a brief, manful effort. But the irrepressible outbursts from the audience bewildered them; every time Sir Lancelot du Lake the Child opened his mouth, the great, shadowy house fell into an uproar, and the children into confusion. Strong women and brave girls in the audience went out into the lobby, shrieking and clinging to one another. Others remained, rocking in their seats, helpless and spent. The neighbourhood of Mrs. Schofield and Margaret became, tactfully, a desert. Friends of the author went behind the scenes and encountered a hitherto unknown phase of Mrs. Lora Rewbush; they said, afterward, that she hardly seemed to know what she was doing. She begged to be left alone somewhere with Penrod Schofield, for just a little while.

They led her away

CHAPTER VI

EVENING

THE sun was setting behind the back fence (though at a considerable distance) as Penrod Schofield approached that fence and looked thoughtfully up at the top of it, apparently having in mind some purpose to climb up and sit there. Debating this, he passed his fingers gently up and down the backs of his legs; and then something seemed to decide him not to sit anywhere. He leaned against the fence, sighed profoundly, and gazed at Duke, his wistful dog.

The sigh was reminiscent: episodes of simple

pathos were passing before his inward eye. About the most painful was the vision of lovely Marjorie Jones, weeping with rage as the Child Sir Lancelot was dragged, insatiate, from the prostrate and howling Child Sir Galahad, after an onslaught delivered the precise instant the curtain began to fall upon the demoralized "pageant." And then — oh, pangs! oh, woman! — she slapped at the ruffian's cheek, as he was led past her by a resentful janitor; and turning, flung her arms round the Child Sir Galahad's neck.

"Penrod Schofield, don't you dare ever speak to me again as long as you live!" Maurice's little white boots and gold tassels had done their work.

At home the late Child Sir Lancelot was consigned to a locked clothes-closet pending the arrival of his father. Mr. Schofield came and, shortly after, there was put into practice an old patriarchal custom. It is a custom of inconceivable antiquity: probably primordial, certainly prehistoric, but still in vogue in some remaining citadels of the ancient simplicities of the Republic.

And now, therefore, in the dusk, Penrod leaned against the fence and sighed.

His case is comparable to that of an adult who

could have survived a similar experience. Looking
back to the sawdust-box, fancy pictures this comparable adult a serious and inventive writer engaged
in congenial literary activities in a private retreat.
We see this period marked by the creation of some
of the most virile passages of a Work dealing exclusively in red corpuscles and huge primal impulses.
We see this thoughtful man dragged from his calm
seclusion to a horrifying publicity; forced to adopt
the stage and, himself a writer, compelled to exploit
the repulsive sentiments of an author not only per-
sonally distasteful to him but whose whole method
and school in *belles lettres* he despises.

We see him reduced by desperation and modesty to
stealing a pair of overalls. We conceive him to have
ruined, then, his own reputation, and to have utterly
disgraced his family; next, to have engaged in the
duello and to have been spurned by his lady-love,
thus lost to him (according to her own declaration)
forever. Finally, we must behold: imprisonment
by the authorities; the third degree — and flagel-
lation.

We conceive our man deciding that his career had
been perhaps too eventful. Yet Penrod had condensed all of it into eight hours.

It appears that he had at least some shadowy perception of a recent fulness of life, for, as he leaned against the fence, gazing upon his wistful Duke, he sighed again and murmured aloud:

"*Well, hasn't this been a day!*"

But in a little while a star came out, freshly lighted, from the highest part of the sky, and Penrod, looking up, noticed it casually and a little drowsily. He yawned. Then he sighed once more, but not reminiscently: evening had come; the day was over.

It was a sigh of pure *ennui*.

CHAPTER VII

EVILS OF DRINK

NEXT day, Penrod acquired a dime by a simple and antique process which was without doubt sometimes practised by the boys of Babylon. When the teacher of his class in Sundayschool requested the weekly contribution, Penrod, fumbling honestly (at first) in the wrong pockets, managed to look so embarrassed that the gentle lady told him not to mind, and said she was often forgetful herself. She was so sweet about it that, looking into the future, Penrod began to feel confident of a small but regular income.

At the close of the afternoon services he did not go home, but proceeded to squander the funds just withheld from China upon an orgy of the most pungently forbidden description. In a Drug Emporium, near the church, he purchased a five-cent sack of candy consisting for the most part of the heavily flavoured hoofs of horned cattle, but undeniably substantial, and so generously capable of resisting solution that the purchaser must needs be avaricious beyond reason who did not realize his money's worth.

Equipped with this collation, Penrod contributed his remaining nickel to a picture show, countenanced upon the seventh day by the legal but not the moral authorities. Here, in cozy darkness, he placidly insulted his liver with jaw-breaker upon jaw-breaker from the paper sack, and in a surfeit of content watched the silent actors on the screen.

One film made a lasting impression upon him. It depicted with relentless pathos the drunkard's progress; beginning with his conversion to beer in the company of loose travelling men; pursuing him through an inexplicable lapse into evening clothes and the society of some remarkably painful ladies; next, exhibiting the effects of alcohol on the victim's domestic disposition, the unfortunate man was seen in the act of striking his wife and, subsequently, his pleading baby daughter with an abnormally heavy walking-stick. Their flight — through the snow — to seek the protection of a relative was shown, and, finally, the drunkard's picturesque behaviour at the portals of a madhouse.

So fascinated was Penrod that he postponed his departure until this film came round again, by which time he had finished his unnatural repast and almost, but not quite, decided against following the profession of a drunkard when he grew up.

Emerging, satiated, from the theatre, a public timepiece before a jeweller's shop confronted him with an unexpected dial and imminent perplexities. How was he to explain at home these hours of dalliance? There was a steadfast rule that he return direct from Sunday-school; and Sunday rules were important, because on that day there was his father, always at home and at hand, perilously ready for action. One of the hardest conditions of boyhood is the almost continuous strain put upon the powers of invention by the constant and harassing necessity for explanations of every natural act.

Proceeding homeward through the deepening twilight as rapidly as possible, at a gait half skip and half canter, Penrod made up his mind in what manner he would account for his long delay, and, as he drew nearer, rehearsed in words the opening passage of his defence.

"Now see here," he determined to begin; "I do not wished to be blamed for things I couldn't help, nor any other boy. I was going along the street by a cottage and a lady put her head out of the window and said her husband was drunk and whipping her and her little girl, and she asked me wouldn't I come in and help hold him. So I went in and tried to get hold of this drunken lady's husband where he was whipping their baby daughter, but he wouldn't pay any attention, and I *told* her I ought to be getting home, but she kep' on askin' me to stay ——"

At this point he reached the corner of his own yard, where a coincidence not only checked the rehearsal of his eloquence but happily obviated all occasion for it. A cab from the station drew up in front of the gate, and there descended a troubled lady in black and a fragile little girl about three. Mrs. Schofield rushed from the house and enfolded both in hospitable arms.

They were Penrod's Aunt Clara and cousin, also Clara, from Dayton, Illinois, and in the flurry of their arrival everybody forgot to put Penrod to the question. It is doubtful, however, if he felt any relief; there may have been even a slight, unconscious disappointment not altogether dissimilar to that of an actor deprived of a good part.

In the course of some really necessary preparations for dinner he stepped from the bathroom into the pink-and-white bedchamber of his sister, and addressed her rather thickly through a towel.

"When'd mamma find out Aunt Clara and Cousin Clara were coming?"

"Not till she saw them from the window. She just happened to look out as they drove up. Aunt Clara telegraphed this morning, but it wasn't delivered."

"How long they goin' to stay?"

"I don't know."

Penrod ceased to rub his shining face, and thoughtfully tossed the towel through the bathroom door. "Uncle John won't try to make 'em come back home, I guess, will he?" (Uncle John was Aunt Clara's husband, a successful manufacturer of stoves, and his lifelong regret was that he had not entered the Baptist ministry.) "He'll let 'em stay here quietly, won't he?"

"What *are* you talking about?" demanded Margaret, turning from her mirror. "Uncle John sent them here. Why shouldn't he let them stay?"

Penrod looked crestfallen. "Then he hasn't taken to drink?"

"Certainly not!" She emphasized the denial with a pretty peal of soprano laughter.

"Then why," asked her brother gloomily, "why did Aunt Clara look so worried when she got here?"

"Good gracious! Don't people worry about anything except somebody's drinking? Where did you get such an idea?"

"Well," he persisted, "you don't *know* it ain't that."

She laughed again, whole-heartedly. "Poor Uncle John! He won't even allow grape juice or ginger ale in his house. They came because they were afraid little Clara might catch the measles. She's very delicate, and there's such an epidemic of measles among the children over in Dayton the schools had to be closed. Uncle John got so worried that last night he dreamed about it; and this morning he couldn't stand it any longer and packed them off over here, though he thinks it's wicked to travel on Sunday. And Aunt Clara was worried when she got here because they'd forgotten to check her trunk and it will have to be sent by express. Now what in the name of the common sense put it into your head that Uncle John had taken to ——"

"Oh, nothing." He turned lifelessly away and went downstairs, a new-born hope dying in his bosom. Life seems so needlessly dull sometimes.

CHAPTER VIII

SCHOOL

NEXT morning, when he had once more resumed the dreadful burden of education,
it seemed infinitely duller. And yet what
pleasanter sight is there than a schoolroom well filled
with children of those sprouting years just before
the 'teens? The casual visitor, gazing from the
teacher's platform upon these busy little heads,
needs only a blunted memory to experience the most
agreeable and exhilarating sensations. Still, for the
greater part, the children are unconscious of the
happiness of their condition; for nothing is more

pathetically true than that we " never know when we
are well off." The boys in a public school are less
aware of their happy state than are the girls; and
of all the boys in his room, probably Penrod himself
had the least appreciation of his felicity.

He sat staring at an open page of a textbook, but
not studyin g; not even reading; not even thinking.
Nor was he lost in a reverie: his mind's eye was
shut, as his physical eye might well have been, for
the optic nerve, flaccid with *ennui*, conveyed nothing
whatever of the printed page upon which the orb of
vision was partially focused. Penrod was doing
something very unusual and rare, something almost
never accomplished except by coloured people or by
a boy in school on a spring day: he was doing really
nothing at all. He was merely a state of being.

From the street a sound stole in through the open
window, and abhorring Nature began to fill the
vacuum called Penrod Schofield; for the sound was
the spring song of a mouth-organ, coming down the
sidewalk. The windows were intentionally above
the level of the eyes of the seated pupils; but the
picture of the musician was plain to Penrod, painted
for him by a quality in the runs and trills partaking
of the oboe, of the calliope, and of cats in anguish;

an excruciating sweetness obtained only by the
wallowing, walloping yellow-pink palm of a hand
whose back was Congo black and shiny. The music
came down the street and passed beneath the window,
accompanied by the care-free shuffling of a pair of
old shoes scuffing syncopations on the cement sidewalk. It passed into the distance; became faint
and blurred; was gone. Emotion stirred in Penrod
a great and poignant desire, but (perhaps fortunately)
no fairy godmother made her appearance. Otherwise Penrod would have gone down the street in a
black skin, playing the mouth-organ, and an unpre-
pared coloured youth would have found himself en-
joying educational advantages for which he had no
ambition whatever.

Roused from perfect apathy, the boy cast about
the schoolroom an eye wearied to nausea by the per-
petual vision of the neat teacher upon the platform,
the backs of the heads of the pupils in front of him,
and the monotonous stretches of blackboard threateningly defaced by arithmetical formulæ and other
insignia of torture. Above the blackboard, the walls
of the high room were of white plaster — white with
the qualified whiteness of old snow in a soft coal
town. This dismal expanse was broken by four,

lithographic portraits, votive offerings of a thoughtful publisher. The portraits were of good and great men, kind men; men who loved children. Their faces were noble and benevolent. But the lithographs offered the only rest for the eyes of children fatigued by the everlasting sameness of the schoolroom. Long day after long day, interminable week in and interminable week out, vast month on vast month, the pupils sat with those four portraits beaming kindness down upon them. The faces became permanent in the consciousness of the children; they became an obsession — in and out of school the children were never free of them. The four faces haunted the minds of children falling asleep; they hung upon the minds of children waking at night; they rose forebodingly in the minds of children waking in the morning; they became monstrously alive in the minds of children lying sick of fever. Never, while the children of that schoolroom lived, would they be able to forget one detail of the four lithographs: the hand of Longfellow was fixed, for them, forever, in his beard. And by a simple and unconscious association of ideas, Penrod Schofield was accumulating an antipathy for the gentle Longfellow and for James Russell Lowell and for Oliver

Wendell Holmes and for John Greenleaf Whittier, which would never permit him to peruse a work of one of those great New Englanders without a feeling of personal resentment.

His eyes fell slowly and inimically from the brow of Whittier to the braid of reddish hair belonging to Victorine Riordan, the little octoroon girl who sat directly in front of him. Victorine's back was as familiar to Penrod as the necktie of Oliver Wendell Holmes. So was her gayly coloured plaid waist. He hated the waist as he hated Victorine herself, without knowing why. Enforced companionship in large quantities and on an equal basis between the sexes appears to sterilize the affections, and school-room romances are few.

Victorine's hair was thick, and the brickish glints in it were beautiful, but Penrod was very tired of it. A tiny knot of green ribbon finished off the braid and kept it from unravelling; and beneath the ribbon there was a final wisp of hair which was just long enough to repose upon Penrod's desk when Victorine leaned back in her seat. It was there now. Thoughtfully, he took the braid between thumb and forefinger, and, without disturbing Victorine, dipped the end of it and the green ribbon into the ink-

well of his desk.   He brought hair and ribbon forth
dripping purple ink, and partially dried them on a
blotter, though, a moment later when Victorine
leaned forward, they were still able to add a few picturesque touches to the plaid waist.

Rudolph Krauss, across the aisle from Penrod,
watched the operation with protuberant eyes, fascinated.   Inspired to imitation, he took a piece of
chalk from his pocket and wrote "*RATS*" across the
shoulder-blades of the boy in front of him, then
looked across appealingly to Penrod for tokens of
congratulation.   Penrod yawned.   It may not be
denied that at times he appeared to be a very self-
centred boy

CHAPTER IX

SOARING

HALF the members of the class passed out to a recitation-room, the empurpled Victorine among them, and Miss Spence started the remaining half through the ordeal of trial by mathematics. Several boys and girls were sent to the blackboard, and Penrod, spared for the moment, followed their operations a little while with his eyes, but not with his mind; then, sinking deeper in his seat, limply abandoned the effort. His eyes remained open, but saw nothing; the routine of the arithmetic lesson reached his ears in familiar, meaningless sounds, but he heard nothing; and yet, this time, he was profoundly occupied. He had drifted away from the painful land of facts, and floated now in a new sea of fancy which he had just discovered.

Maturity forgets the marvellous realness of a boy's day-dreams, how colourful they glow, rosy and living, and how opaque the curtain closing down between the dreamer and the actual world. That curtain is almost sound-proof, too, and causes more throat-trouble among parents than is suspected.

The nervous monotony of the schoolroom inspires a sometimes unbearable longing for something astonishing to happen, and as every boy's fundamental desire is to do something astonishing himself, so as to be the centre of all human interest and awe, it was natural that Penrod should discover in fancy the delightful secret of self-levitation. He found, in this curious series of imaginings, during the lesson in arithmetic, that the atmosphere may be navigated as by a swimmer under water, but with infinitely greater ease and with perfect comfort in breathing. In his mind he extended his arms gracefully, at a level with his shoulders, and delicately paddled the air with his hands, which at once caused him to be drawn up out of his seat and elevated gently to a position about midway between the floor and the ceiling, where he came to an equilibrium and floated; a sensation not the less exquisite because of the screams of his fellow pupils, appalled by the miracle. Miss Spence herself was amazed and frightened, but he only smiled down carelessly upon her when she commanded him to return to earth; and then, when she climbed upon a desk to pull him down, he quietly paddled himself a little higher, leaving his toes just out of her reach. Next, he swam through a few slow somersaults to show his mastery of the new art, and, with the shouting of the dumfounded scholars ringing in his ears, turned on his side and floated swiftly out of the window, immediately rising above the housetops, while people in the street below him shrieked, and a trolley car stopped dead in wonder.

With almost no exertion he paddled himself, many yards at a stroke, to the girls' private school where Marjorie Jones was a pupil — Marjorie Jones of the amber curls and the golden voice! Long before the "Pageant of the Table Round," she had offered Penrod a hundred proofs that she considered him wholly undesirable and ineligible. At the Friday Afternoon Dancing Class she consistently incited and led the laughter at him whenever Professor Bartet singled him out for admonition in matters of feet and decorum. And but yesterday she had chid him for his slavish lack of memory in daring to offer her greeting on the way to Sunday-school. "Well! I expect you must forgot I told you never to speak to me again! If I was a boy, I'd be too proud to come hanging around people that don't speak to me, even if I *was* the Worst Boy in Town!" So she flouted him. But now, as he floated in through the window of her classroom and swam gently along the ceiling like an escaped toy balloon, she fell upon her knees beside her little desk, and, lifting up her arms toward him, cried with love and admiration:

"Oh, *Pen*rod!"

He negligently kicked a globe from the high chandelier, and, smiling coldly, floated out through the hall to the front steps of the school, while Marjorie followed, imploring him to grant her one kind look.

In the street an enormous crowd had gathered, headed by Miss Spence and a brass band; and a cheer from a hundred thousand throats shook the very ground as Penrod swam overhead. Marjorie knelt upon the steps and watched adoringly while Penrod took the drum-major's baton and, performing sinuous evolutions above the crowd, led the band. Then he threw the baton so high that it disappeared from sight; but he went swiftly after it, a double delight, for he had not only the delicious sensation of rocketing safely up and up into the blue sky, but also that of standing in the crowd below, watching and admiring himself as he dwindled to a speck, disappeared, and then, emerging from a cloud, came speeding down, with the baton in his hand, to the level of the treetops, where he beat time for the band and the vast throng and Marjorie Jones, who all united in the "Star-spangled Banner" in honour of his aerial achievements. It was a great moment.

It was a great moment, but something seemed to threaten it. The face of Miss Spence looking up from the crowd grew too vivid — unpleasantly vivid. She was beckoning him and shouting, "Come down, Penrod Schofield! Penrod Schofield, come down here!" He could hear her above the band and the singing of the multitude; she seemed intent on spoiling everything. Marjorie Jones was weeping to show how sorry she was that she had formerly slighted him, and throwing kisses to prove that she loved him; but Miss Spence kept jumping between him and Marjorie, incessantly calling his name.

He grew more and more irritated with her; he was the most important person in the world and was engaged in proving it to Marjorie Jones and the whole city, and yet Miss Spence seemed to feel she still had the right to order him about as she did in the old days when he was an ordinary schoolboy. He was furious; he was sure she wanted him to do something disagreeable. It seemed to him that she had screamed "Penrod Schofield!" thousands of times.

From the beginning of his aerial experiments in his own schoolroom, he had not opened his lips, knowing somehow that one of the requirements for air floating is perfect silence on the part of the floater; but, finally, irritated beyond measure by Miss Spence's clamorous insistence, he was unable to restrain an indignant rebuke — and immediately came to earth with a frightful bump.

Miss Spence — in the flesh — had directed toward the physical body of the absent Penrod an inquiry as to the fractional consequences of dividing seventeen apples, fairly, among three boys, and she was surprised and displeased to receive no answer although to the best of her knowledge and belief, he was looking fixedly at her. She repeated her question crisply, without visible effect; then summoned him by name with increasing asperity. Twice she called him, while all his fellow pupils turned to stare at the gazing boy. She advanced a step from the platform.

"Penrod Schofield!"

"Oh, my goodness!" he shouted suddenly. "Can't you keep still a *minute?*"

CHAPTER X

UNCLE JOHN

MISS SPENCE gasped. So did the pupils. The whole room filled with a swelling conglomerate "*O-o-o-o-h!*"

As for Penrod himself, the walls reeled with the shock. He sat with his mouth open, a mere lump of stupefaction. For the appalling words that he had hurled at the teacher were as inexplicable to him as to any other who heard them.

Nothing is more treacherous than the human mind; nothing else so loves to play the Iscariot. Even when patiently bullied into a semblance of order and

71

training, it may prove but a base and shifty servant. And Penrod's mind was not his servant; it was a master, with the April wind's whims; and it had just played him a diabolical trick. The very jolt with which he came back to the schoolroom in the midst of his fancied flight jarred his day-dream utterly out of him; and he sat, open-mouthed in horror at what he had said.

The unanimous gasp of awe was protracted. Miss Spence, however, finally recovered her breath, and, returning deliberately to the platform, faced the school. "And then, for a little while," as pathetic stories sometimes recount, "everything was very still." It was so still, in fact, that Penrod's new-born notoriety could almost be heard growing. This grisly silence was at last broken by the teacher.

"Penrod Schofield, stand up!"

The miserable child obeyed.

"What did you mean by speaking to me in that way?"

He hung his head, raked the floor with the side of his shoe, swayed, swallowed, looked suddenly at his hands with the air of never having seen them before, then clasped them behind him. The school shivered in ecstatic horror, every fascinated eye upon him; yet there was not a soul in the room but was profoundly grateful to him for the sensation — including the offended teacher herself. Unhappily, all this gratitude was unconscious and altogether different from the kind which results in testimonials and loving-cups. On the contrary!

"Penrod Schofield!"

He gulped.

"Answer me at once! Why did you speak to me like that?"

"I was ——" He choked, unable to continue.

"Speak out!"

"I was just — thinking," he managed to stammer.

"That will not do," she returned sharply. "I wish to know immediately why you spoke as you did."

The stricken Penrod answered helplessly:

"Because I was just thinking."

Upon the very rack he could have offered no ampler truthful explanation. It was all he knew about it.

"Thinking what?"

"Just thinking."

Miss Spence's expression gave evidence that her power of self-restraint was undergoing a remarkable test. However, after taking counsel with herself, she commanded:

"Come here!"

He shuffled forward, and she placed a chair upon
the platform near her own.

"Sit there!"

Then (but not at all as if nothing had happened)
she continued the lesson in arithmetic. Spiritually,
the children may have learned a lesson in very small
fractions indeed as they gazed at the fragment of sin
before them on the stool of penitence. They all
stared at him attentively with hard and passionately interested eyes, in which there was never one
trace of pity. It cannot be said with precision that
he writhed; his movement was more a slow, continuous squirm, effected with a ghastly assumption
of languid indifference; while his gaze, in the effort
to escape the marble-hearted glare of his schoolmates,
affixed itself with apparent permanence to the waistcoat button of James Russell Lowell just above the
"u" in "Russell."

Classes came and classes went, grilling him with
eyes. Newcomers received the story of the crime
in darkling whispers; and the outcast sat and sat
and sat, and squirmed and squirmed and squirmed.
(He did one or two things with his spine which
a professional contortionist would have observed

The outcast sat, and sat and sat, and squirmed, and squirmed and squirmed

with real interest.) And all this while of freezing suspense was but the criminal's detention awaiting trial. A known punishment may be anticipated with some measure of equanimity; at least, the prisoner may prepare himself to undergo it; but the unknown looms more monstrous for every attempt to guess it. Penrod's crime was unique; there were no rules to aid him in estimating the vengeance to fall upon him for it. What seemed most probable was that he would be expelled from the schools in the presence of his family, the mayor, and council, and afterward whipped by his father upon the State House steps, with the entire city as audience by invitation of the authorities.

Noon came. The rows of children filed out, every head turning for a last unpleasingly speculative look at the outlaw. Then Miss Spence closed the door into the cloakroom and that into the big hall, and came and sat at her desk, near Penrod. The tramping of feet outside, the shrill calls and shouting and the changing voices of the older boys ceased to be heard — and there was silence. Penrod, still affecting to be occupied with Lowell, was conscious that Miss Spence looked at him intently.

"Penrod," she said gravely, "what excuse have

you to offer before I report your case to the principal?"

The word "principal" struck him to the vitals. Grand Inquisitor, Grand Khan, Sultan, Emperor, Tsar, Cæsar Augustus— these are comparable. He stopped squirming instantly, and sat rigid.

"I want an answer. Why did you shout those words at me?"

"Well," he murmured, "I was just — thinking."

"Thinking what?" she asked sharply.

"I don't know."

"That won't do!"

He took his left ankle in his right hand and regarded it helplessly.

"That won't do, Penrod Schofield," she repeated severely. "If that is all the excuse you have to offer I shall report your case this instant!"

And she rose with fatal intent.

But Penrod was one of those whom the precipice inspires. "Well, I *have* got an excuse."

"Well" — she paused impatiently — "what is it?"

He had not an idea, but he felt one coming, and replied automatically, in a plaintive tone:

"I guess anybody that had been through what *I*

had to go through, last night, would think they had an excuse."

Miss Spence resumed her seat, though with the air of being ready to leap from it instantly.

"What has last night to do with your insolence to me this morning?"

"Well, I guess you'd see," he returned, emphasizing the plaintive note, "if you knew what *I* know."

"Now, Penrod," she said, in a kinder voice, "I have a high regard for your mother and father, and it would hurt me to distress them, but you must either tell me what was the matter with you or I'll have to take you to Mrs. Houston."

"Well, ain't I going to?" he cried, spurred by the dread name. "It's because I didn't sleep last night."

"Were you ill?" The question was put with some dryness.

He felt the dryness. "No'm; *I* wasn't."

"Then if some one in your family was so ill that even you were kept up all night, how does it happen they let you come to school this morning?"

"It wasn't illness," he returned, shaking his head mournfully. "It was lots worse'n anybody's being sick. It was — it was — well, it was jest awful."

"*What* was?" He marked with anxiety the incredulity in her tone.

"It was about Aunt Clara," he said.

"Your Aunt Clara!" she repeated. "Do you mean your mother's sister who married Mr. Farry of Dayton, Illinois?"

"Yes — Uncle John," returned Penrod sorrowfully. "The trouble was about him."

Miss Spence frowned a frown which he rightly interpreted as one of continued suspicion. "She and I were in school together," she said. "I used to know her very well, and I've always heard her married life was entirely happy. I don't ——"

"Yes, it was," he interrupted, "until last year when Uncle John took to running with travelling men ——"

"What?"

"Yes'm." He nodded solemnly. "That was what started it. At first he was a good, kind husband, but these travelling men would coax him into a saloon on his way from work, and they got him to drinking beer and then ales, wines, liquors, and cigars ——"

"Penrod!"

"Ma'am?"

"I'm not inquiring into your Aunt Clara's private

affairs; I'm asking you if you have anything to say which would palliate ——"

"That's what I'm tryin' to *tell* you about, Miss Spence," he pleaded, — "if you'd jest only let me. When Aunt Clara and her little baby daughter got to our house last night ——"

"You say Mrs. Farry is visiting your mother?"

"Yes'm — not just visiting — you see, she *had* to come. Well of course, little baby Clara, she was so bruised up and mauled, where he'd been hittin' her with his cane ——"

"You mean that your uncle had done such a thing as *that!*" exclaimed Miss Spence, suddenly disarmed by this scandal.

"Yes'm, and mamma and Margaret had to sit up all night nursin' little Clara — and *Aunt* Clara was in such a state *somebody* had to keep talkin' to *her*, and there wasn't anybody but me to do it, so I ——"

"But where was your father?" she cried.

"Ma'am?"

"Where was your father while ——"

"Oh — papa?" Penrod paused, reflected; then brightened. "Why, he was down at the train, waitin' to see if Uncle John would try to follow 'em and make 'em come home so's he could persecute 'em some more. I wanted to do that, but they said if he did come I mightn't be strong enough to hold him, and ——" The brave lad paused again, modestly. Miss Spence's expression was encouraging. Her eyes were wide with astonishment, and there may have been in them, also, the mingled beginnings of admiration and self-reproach. Penrod, warming to his work, felt safer every moment.

"And so," he continued, "I had to sit up with Aunt Clara. She had some pretty big bruises, too, and I had to ——"

"But why didn't they send for a doctor?" However, this question was only a flicker of dying incredulity.

"Oh, they didn't want any *doctor*," exclaimed the inspired realist promptly. "They don't want anybody to *hear* about it because Uncle John might reform — and then where'd he be if everybody knew he'd been a drunkard and whipped his wife and baby daughter?"

"Oh!" said Miss Spence.

"You see, he used to be upright as anybody," he went on explanatively. "It all begun ——"

"Began, Penrod."

"Yes'm. It all commenced from the first day he let those travelling men coax him into the saloon."

Penrod narrated the downfall of his Uncle John at length. In detail he was nothing short of plethoric; and incident followed incident, sketched with such vividness, such abundance of colour, and such verisimilitude to a drunkard's life as a drunkard's life should be, that had Miss Spence possessed the rather chilling attributes of William J. Burns himself, the last trace of skepticism must have vanished from her mind. Besides, there are two things that will be believed of any man whatsoever, and one of them is that he has taken to drink. And in every sense it was a moving picture which, with simple but eloquent words, the virtuous Penrod set before his teacher.

His eloquence increased with what it fed on; and as with the eloquence so with self-reproach in the gentle bosom of the teacher. She cleared her throat with difficulty once or twice, during his description of his ministering night with Aunt Clara. "And I said to her, 'Why, Aunt Clara, what's the use of takin' on so about it?' And I said, 'Now Aunt Clara all the crying in the world can't make things any better.' And then she'd just keep catchin' hold of me, and sob and kind of holler, and I'd say, '*Don't* cry, Aunt Clara — *please* don't cry.'"

Then, under the influence of some fragmentary

survivals of the respectable portion of his Sunday
adventures, his theme became more exalted; and,
only partially misquoting a phrase from a psalm,
he related how he had made it of comfort to Aunt
Clara, and how he had besought her to seek Higher
guidance in her trouble.

The surprising thing about a structure such as
Penrod was erecting is that the taller it becomes the
more ornamentation it will stand. Gifted boys
have this faculty of building magnificence upon cobwebs — and Penrod was gifted. Under the spell
of his really great performance, Miss Spence gazed
more and more sweetly upon the prodigy of spiritual
beauty and goodness before her, until at last, when
Penrod came to the explanation of his "just thinking," she was forced to turn her head away.

"You mean, dear," she said gently, "that you were
all worn out and hardly knew what you were saying?"

"Yes'm."

"And you were thinking about all those dreadful
things so hard that you forgot where you were?"

"I was thinking," he said simply, "how to save
Uncle John."

And the end of it for this mighty boy was that the
teacher kissed him!

CHAPTER XI

FIDELITY OF A LITTLE DOG

THE returning students, that afternoon, observed that Penrod's desk was vacant — and nothing could have been more impressive than that sinister mere emptiness. The accepted theory was that Penrod had been arrested. How breath-taking then, the sensation when, at the beginning of the second hour, he strolled in with inimitable carelessness and, rubbing his eyes, somewhat noticeably in the manner of one who has snatched an hour of much needed sleep, took his place as if nothing in particular had happened. This, at first supposed to be a superhuman exhibition of sheer audacity, became but the more dumfounding when Miss Spence — looking up from her desk — greeted him with a pleasant little nod. Even after school, Penrod gave numerous maddened investigators no relief. All he would consent to say was:

"Oh, I just *talked* to her."

A mystification not entirely unconnected with the one thus produced was manifested at his own family dinner-table the following evening. Aunt Clara had been out rather late, and came to the table after the rest were seated. She wore a puzzled expression.

"Do you ever see Mary Spence nowadays?" she inquired, as she unfolded her napkin, addressing Mrs. Schofield. Penrod abruptly set down his soup-spoon and gazed at his aunt with flattering attention.

"Yes; sometimes," said Mrs. Schofield. "She's Penrod's teacher."

"Is she?" said Mrs. Farry. "Do you —" She paused. "Do people think her a little — queer, these days?"

"Why, no," returned her sister. "What makes you say that?"

"She has acquired a very odd manner," said Mrs.

Farry decidedly. "At least, she seemed odd to *me*. I met her at the corner just before I got to the house, a few minutes ago, and after we'd said howdy-do to each other, she kept hold of my hand and looked as though she was going to cry. She seemed to be trying to say something, and choking ——"

"But I don't think that's so very queer, Clara. She knew you in school, didn't she?"

"Yes, but ——"

"And she hadn't seen you for so many years, I think it's perfectly natural she ——"

"Wait! She stood there squeezing my hand, and struggling to get her voice — and I got really embarrassed — and then finally she said, in a kind of tearful whisper, 'Be of good cheer — this trial will pass!'"

"How queer!" exclaimed Margaret.

Penrod sighed, and returned somewhat absently to his soup.

"Well, I don't know," said Mrs. Schofield thoughtfully. "Of course she's heard about the outbreak of measles in Dayton, since they had to close the schools, and she knows you live there ——"

"But doesn't it seem a *very* exaggerated way," suggested Margaret, "to talk about measles?"

"Wait!" begged Aunt Clara. "After she said that, she said something even queerer, and then put her handkerchief to her eyes and hurried away."

Penrod laid down his spoon again and moved his chair slightly back from the table. A spirit of prophecy was upon him: he knew that some one was going to ask a question which he felt might better remain unspoken.

"What *was* the other thing she said?" Mr. Schofield inquired, thus immediately fulfilling his son's premonition.

"She said," returned Mrs. Farry slowly, looking about the table, "she said, 'I know that Penrod is a great, great comfort to you!'"

There was a general exclamation of surprise. It was a singular thing, and in no manner may it be considered complimentary to Penrod, that this speech of Miss Spence's should have immediately confirmed Mrs. Farry's doubts about her in the minds of all his family.

Mr. Schofield shook his head pityingly.

"I'm afraid she's a goner," he went so far as to say.

"Of all the weird ideas!" cried Margaret.

"I never heard anything like it in my life!" Mrs. Schofield exclaimed. "Was that *all* she said?"

"Every word!"

Penrod again resumed attention to his soup. His mother looked at him curiously, and then, struck by a sudden thought, gathered the glances of the adults of the table by a significant movement of the head, and, by another, conveyed an admonition to drop the subject until later. Miss Spence was Penrod's teacher: it was better for many reasons, not to discuss the subject of her queerness before him. This was Mrs. Schofield's thought at the time. Later she had another, and it kept her awake.

The next afternoon, Mr. Schofield, returning at five o'clock from the cares of the day, found the house deserted, and sat down to read his evening paper in what appeared to be an uninhabited apartment known to its own world as the "drawing-room." A sneeze, unexpected both to him and the owner, informed him of the presence of another person.

"Where are you, Penrod?" the parent asked, looking about.

"Here," said Penrod meekly.

Stooping, Mr. Schofield discovered his son squatting under the piano, near an open window — his wistful Duke lying beside him.

"What are you doing there?"

"Me?"

"Why under the piano?"

"Well," the boy returned, with grave sweetness, "I was just kind of sitting here — thinking."

"All right." Mr. Schofield, rather touched, returned to the digestion of a murder, his back once more to the piano; and Penrod silently drew from beneath his jacket (where he had slipped it simultaneously with the sneeze) a paper-backed volume entitled: "Slimsy, the Sioux City Squealer, or, 'Not Guilty, Your Honor.'"

In this manner the reading-club continued in peace, absorbed, contented, the world well forgot — until a sudden, violently irritated slam-bang of the front door startled the members; and Mrs. Schofield burst into the room and threw herself into a chair, moaning.

"What's the matter, mamma?" asked her husband, laying aside his paper.

"Henry Passloe Schofield," returned the lady, "I don't know what *is* to be done with that boy; I do *not!*"

"You mean Penrod?"

"Who else could I mean?" She sat up, exasperated, to stare at him. "Henry Passloe Schofield, you've got to take this matter in your hands — it's beyond me!"

"Well, what has he ——"

"Last night I got to thinking," she began rapidly, "about what Clara told us — thank heaven she and Margaret and little Clara have gone to tea at Cousin Charlotte's! — but they'll be home soon — about what she said about Miss Spence ——"

"You mean about Penrod's being a comfort?"

"Yes, and I kept thinking and thinking and thinking about it till I couldn't stand it any ——"

"By *George!*" shouted Mr. Schofield startlingly, stooping to look under the piano. A statement that he had suddenly remembered his son's presence would be lacking in accuracy, for the highly sensitized Penrod was, in fact, no longer present. No more was Duke, his faithful dog.

"What's the matter?"

"Nothing," he returned, striding to the open window and looking out. "Go on."

"Oh," she moaned, "it must be kept from Clara — and I'll never hold up my head again if John Farry ever hears of it!"

"Hears of *what?*"

"Well, I just couldn't stand it, I got so curious;

and I thought of course if Miss Spence *had* become a little unbalanced it was my duty to know it, as Penrod's mother and she his teacher; so I thought I would just call on her at her apartment after school and have a chat and see — and I did and — oh ——"

"Well?"

"I've just come from there, and she told me — she told me! Oh, I've *never* known anything like this!"

"*What* did she tell you?"

Mrs. Schofield, making a great effort, managed to assume a temporary appearance of calm. "Henry," she said solemnly, "bear this in mind: whatever you do to Penrod, it must be done in some place when Clara won't hear it. But the first thing to do is to find him."

Within view of the window from which Mr. Schofield was gazing was the closed door of the storeroom in the stable, and just outside this door Duke was performing a most engaging trick.

His young master had taught Duke to "sit up and beg" when he wanted anything, and if that didn't get it, to "speak." Duke was facing the closed door and sitting up and begging, and now he also spoke — in a loud, clear bark.

There was an open transom over the door, and from this descended — hurled by an unseen agency— a can half filled with old paint.

It caught the small besieger of the door on his thoroughly surprised right ear, encouraged him to some remarkable acrobatics, and turned large portions of him a dull blue. Allowing only a moment to perplexity, and deciding, after a single and evidently unappetizing experiment, not to cleanse himself of paint, the loyal animal resumed his quaint, upright posture.

Mr. Schofield seated himself on the window-sill, whence he could keep in view that pathetic picture of unrequited love.

"Go on with your story, mamma," he said. "I think I can find Penrod when we want him."

And a few minutes later he added, "And I think I know the place to do it in."

Again the faithful voice of Duke was heard, pleading outside the bolted door.

CHAPTER XII

MISS RENNSDALE ACCEPTS

"ONE-TWO-THREE; one-two-three—glide!" said Professor Bartet, emphasizing his instructions by a brisk collision of his palms at "glide." "One-two-three; one-two-three— glide!"

The school week was over, at last, but Penrod's troubles were not.

Round and round the ballroom went the seventeen struggling little couples of the Friday Afternoon Dancing Class. Round and round went their reflections with them, swimming rhythmically in the polished, dark floor — white and blue and pink for the girls; black, with dabs of white, for the white-collared, white-gloved boys; and sparks and slivers of high light everywhere as the glistening pumps flickered along the surface like a school of flying fish. Every small pink face — with one exception — was painstaking and set for duty. It was a conscientious little merry-go-round.

"One-two-three; one-two-three — glide! One-two-three; one-two-three — glide! One-two-th —— Ha! Mister Penrod Schofield, you lose the step. Your left foot! No, no! This is the left! See — like me! Now again! One-two-three; one-two-three — glide! Better! Much better! Again! One-two-three; one-two-three — gl —— Stop! **Mr.** Penrod Schofield, this dancing class is provided by the kind parents of the pupilses as much to learn the mannerss of good societies as to dance. You think you shall ever see a gentleman in good societies to tickle his partner in the dance till she say Ouch? Never! I assure you it is not done. Again! Now then! Piano, please! One-two-three; one-two-three — glide! **Mr.** Penrod Schofield, your right foot — your right foot! No, no! Stop!"

The merry-go-round came to a standstill.

"Mr. Penrod Schofield and partner" — Professor

Bartet wiped his brow — "will you kindly observe me? One-two-three — glide! So! Now then — no; you will please keep your places, ladies and gentlemen. Mr. Penrod Schofield, I would puttickly like your attention; this is for you!"

"Pickin' on me again!" murmured the smouldering Penrod to his small, unsympathetic partner. "Can't let me alone a minute!"

"Mister Georgie Bassett, please step to the centre," said the professor.

Mr. Bassett complied with modest alacrity.

"Teacher's pet!" whispered Penrod hoarsely. He had nothing but contempt for Georgie Bassett. The parents, guardians, aunts, uncles, cousins, governesses, housemaids, cooks, chauffeurs and coachmen, appertaining to the members of the dancing class, all dwelt in the same part of town and shared certain communal theories; and among the most firmly established was that which maintained Georgie Bassett to be the Best Boy in Town. Contrariwise, the unfortunate Penrod, largely because of his recent dazzling but disastrous attempts to control forces far beyond him, had been given a clear title as the Worst Boy in Town. (Population, 135,000.) To precisely what degree his reputation

was the product of his own energies cannot be cal-
culated. It was Marjorie Jones who first applied
the description, in its definite simplicity, the day
after the "pageant," and, possibly, her frequent and
effusive repetitions of it, even upon wholly irrelevant
occasions, had something to do with its prompt and
quite perfect acceptance by the community.

"Miss Rennsdale will please do me the fafer to
be Mr. Georgie Bassett's partner for one moment,"
said Professor Bartet. "Mr. Penrod Schofield will
please give his attention. Miss Rennsdale and
Mister Bassett, obliche me, if you please. Others
please watch. Piano, please! Now then!"

Miss Rennsdale, aged eight — the youngest lady
in the class — and Mr. Georgie Bassett one-two-
three-glided with consummate technique for the
better education of Penrod Schofield. It is possible that amber-curled, beautiful Marjorie felt that
she, rather than Miss Rennsdale, might have been
selected as the example of perfection — or perhaps
her remark was only woman.

"Stopping everybody for that boy!" said Marjorie.

Penrod, across the circle from her, heard distinctly
— nay, he was obviously intended to hear; but over
a scorched heart he preserved a stoic front. Where-

upon Marjorie whispered derisively in the ear of her partner, Maurice Levy, who wore a pearl pin in his tie.

"Again, please, everybody — ladies and gentlemen!" cried Professor Bartet. "Mister Penrod Schofield, if you please, pay puttickly attention! Piano, please! Now then!"

The lesson proceeded. At the close of the hour Professor Bartet stepped to the centre of the room and clapped his hands for attention.

"Ladies and gentlemen, if you please to seat yourselves quietly," he said; "I speak to you now about to-morrow. As you all know —— Mister Penrod Schofield, I am not sticking up in a tree outside that window!   If you do me the fafer to examine I am here, insides of the room. Now then! Piano, pl — no, I do not wish the piano! As you all know, this is the last lesson of the season until next October. To-morrow is our special afternoon; beginning three o'clock, we dance the cotillon. But this afternoon comes the test of mannerss. You must see if each know how to make a little formal call like a grown-up people in good societies. You have had good, perfect instruction; let us see if we know how to perform like societies ladies and gentlemen twenty-six years of age.

"Now, when you are dismissed each lady will go to her home and prepare to receive a call. The gentlemen will allow the ladies time to reach their houses and to prepare to receive callers; then each gentleman will call upon a lady and beg the pleasure to engage her for a partner in the cotillon to-morrow. You all know the correct, proper form for these calls, because didn't I work teaching you last lesson till I thought I would drop dead? Yes! Now each gentleman, if he reach a lady's house behind some other gentleman, then he must go somewhere else to a lady's house, and keep calling until he secures a partner; so, as there are the same number of both, everybody shall have a partner.

"Now please all remember that if in case —— Mister Penrod Schofield, when you make your call on a lady I beg you please remember that gentlemen in good societies do not scratch the back in societies as you appear to attempt; so please allow the hands to rest carelessly in the lap. Now please all remember that if in case —— Mister Penrod Schofield, if you please! Gentlemen in societies do not scratch the back by causing frictions between it and the back of your chair, either! Nobody else is itching here! *I* do not itch! I cannot talk if you must itch! In the name of Heaven, why must you always itch? What was I saying? Where — ah! the cotillon — yes! For the cotillon it is important nobody shall fail to be here to-morrow; but if any one should be so very ill he cannot possible come he must write a very polite note of regrets in the form of good societies to his engaged partner to excuse himself — and he must give the reason.

"I do not think anybody is going to be that sick to-morrow — no; and I will find out and report to parents if anybody would try it and not be. But it is important for the cotillon that we have an even number of so many couples, and if it should happen that some one comes and her partner has sent her a polite note that he has genuine reasons why he cannot come, the note must be handed at once to me, so that I arrange some other partner. Is all understood? Yes. The gentlemen will remember now to allow the ladies plenty of time to reach their houses and prepare to receive calls. Ladies and gentlemen, I thank you for your polite attention."

It was nine blocks to the house of Marjorie Jones; but Penrod did it in less than seven minutes from a flying start — such was his haste to lay himself and his hand for the cotillon at the feet of one who had so recently spoken unamiably of him in public. He had not yet learned that the only safe male rebuke to a scornful female is to stay away from her — especially if that is what she desires. However, he did not wish to rebuke her; simply and ardently he wished to dance the cotillon with her. Resentment was swallowed up in hope.

The fact that Miss Jones' feeling for him bore a striking resemblance to that of Simon Legree for Uncle Tom, deterred him not at all. Naturally, he was not wholly unconscious that when he should lay his hand for the cotillon at her feet it would be her inward desire to step on it; but he believed that if he were first in the field Marjorie would have to accept. These things are governed by law.

It was his fond intention to reach her house even in advance of herself, and with grave misgiving he beheld a large automobile at rest before the sainted gate. Forthwith, a sinking feeling became a portent inside him as little Maurice Levy emerged from the front door of the house.

" 'Lo, Penrod!" said Maurice airily.

"What you doin' in there?" inquired Penrod.

"In where?"

"In Marjorie's."

"Well, what shouldn't I be doin' in Marjorie's?" Mr. Levy returned indignantly. "I was inviting her for my partner in the cotillon — what you s'pose?"

"You haven't got any right to!" Penrod protested hotly. "You can't do it yet."

"I did do it yet!" said Maurice.

"You can't!" insisted Penrod. "You got to allow them time first. He said the ladies had to be allowed time to prepare."

"Well, ain't she had time to prepare?"

"When?" Penrod demanded, stepping close to his rival threateningly. "I'd like to know when ——"

"When?" echoed the other with shrill triumph. "When? Why, in mamma's sixty-horse powder limousine automobile, what Marjorie came home with me in! I guess that's when!"

An impulse in the direction of violence became visible upon the countenance of Penrod.

"I expect you need some wiping down," he began dangerously. "I'll give you sumpthing to re-mem ——"

"Oh, you will!" Maurice cried with astonishing truculence, contorting himself into what he may have considered a posture of defense. "Let's see you try it, you — you itcher!"

For the moment, defiance from such a source was dumfounding. Then, luckily, Penrod recollected something and glanced at the automobile.

Perceiving therein not only the alert chauffeur but the magnificent outlines of Mrs. Levy, his enemy's mother, he manœuvred his lifted hand so that it seemed he had but meant to scratch his ear.

"Well, I guess I better be goin'," he said casually. "See you t'-morrow!"

Maurice mounted to the lap of luxury, and Penrod strolled away with an assumption of careless ease which was put to a severe strain when, from the rear window of the car, a sudden protuberance in the nature of a small, dark, curly head shrieked scornfully:

"Go on — you big stiff!"

The cotillon loomed dismally before Penrod now; but it was his duty to secure a partner and he set about it with a dreary heart. The delay occasioned by his fruitless attempt on Marjorie and the altercation with his enemy at her gate had allowed other ladies ample time to prepare for callers — and to receive them. Sadly he went from house to house, finding that he had been preceded in one after the other. Altogether his hand for the cotillon was declined eleven times that afternoon on the legitimate ground of previous engagement. This, with Marjorie, scored off all except five of the seventeen possible partners; and four of the five were also sealed away from him, as he learned in chance encounters with other boys upon the street.

One lady alone remained; he bowed to the inevitable and entered this lorn damsel's gate at twilight with an air of great discouragement. The lorn damsel was Miss Rennsdale, aged eight.

We are apt to forget that there are actually times of life when too much youth is a handicap. Miss Rennsdale was beautiful; she danced like a première; she had every charm but age. On that account alone had she been allowed so much time to prepare to receive callers that it was only by the most manful efforts she could keep her lip from trembling.

A decorous maid conducted the long-belated applicant to her where she sat upon a sofa beside a nursery governess. The decorous maid announced him composedly as he made his entrance.

"Mr. Penrod Schofield!"

Miss Rennsdale suddenly burst into loud sobs.

"Oh!" she wailed. "I just knew it would be him!"

The decorous maid's composure vanished at once

— likewise her decorum. She clapped her hand over her mouth and fled, uttering sounds. The governess, however, set herself to comfort her heartbroken charge, and presently succeeded in restoring Miss Rennsdale to a semblance of that poise with which a lady receives callers and accepts invitations to dance cotillons. But she continued to sob at intervals.

Feeling himself at perhaps a disadvantage, Penrod made offer of his hand for the morrow with a little embarrassment. Following the form prescribed by Professor Bartet, he advanced several paces toward the stricken lady and bowed formally.

"I hope," he said by rote, "you're well, and your parents also in good health. May I have the pleasure of dancing the cotillon as your partner t'-morrow afternoon?"

The wet eyes of Miss Rennsdale searched his countenance without pleasure, and a shudder wrung her small shoulders; but the governess whispered to her instructively, and she made a great effort.

"I thu-thank you fu-for your polite invu-invu-invutation; and I ac ——" Thus far she progressed when emotion overcame her again. She beat frantically upon the sofa with fists and heels. "Oh, I *did* want it to be Georgie Bassett!"

Following the form prescribed by Professor Bartet, he advanced several paces toward the stricken lady, and bowed formally

"No, no, no!" said the governess, and whispered urgently, whereupon Miss Rennsdale was able to complete her acceptance.

"And I ac-accept wu-with pu-pleasure!" she moaned, and immediately, uttering a loud yell, flung herself face downward upon the sofa, clutching her governess convulsively.

Somewhat disconcerted, Penrod bowed again.

"I thank you for your polite acceptance," he murmured hurriedly; "and I trust — I trust — I forget. Oh, yes — I trust we shall have a most enjoyable occasion. Pray present my compliments to your parents; and I must now wish you a very good afternoon."

Concluding these courtly demonstrations with another bow he withdrew in fair order, though thrown into partial confusion in the hall by a final wail from his crushed hostess:

"Oh! Why couldn't it be anybody but *him!*"

CHAPTER XIII

THE SMALLPOX MEDICINE

NEXT morning Penrod woke in profound depression of spirit, the cotillon ominous before him. He pictured Marjorie Jones and Maurice, graceful and light-hearted, flitting by him fairylike, loosing silvery laughter upon him as he engaged in the struggle to keep step with a partner about four years and two feet his junior. It was hard enough for Penrod to keep step with a girl of his size.

The foreboding vision remained with him, increasing in vividness, throughout the forenoon. He found himself unable to fix his mind upon anything else, and, having bent his gloomy footsteps toward the sawdust-box, after breakfast, presently descended therefrom, abandoning Harold Ramorez where he had left him the preceding Saturday. Then, as he sat communing silently with wistful Duke, in the storeroom, coquettish fortune looked his way.

It was the habit of Penrod's mother not to throw away anything whatsoever until years of storage conclusively proved there would never be a use for it; but a recent house-cleaning had ejected upon the back porch a great quantity of bottles and other paraphernalia of medicine, left over from illnesses in the family during a period of several years. This débris Della, the cook, had collected in a large market basket, adding to it some bottles of flavouring extracts that had proved unpopular in the household; also, old catsup bottles; a jar or two of preserves gone bad; various rejected dental liquids — and other things. And she carried the basket out to the storeroom in the stable.

Penrod was at first unaware of what lay before him. Chin on palms, he sat upon the iron rim of a former aquarium and stared morbidly through the open door at the checkered departing back of Della. It was another who saw treasure in the basket she had left.

Mr. Samuel Williams, aged eleven, and congenial to Penrod in years, sex, and disposition, appeared in the doorway, shaking into foam a black liquid within a pint bottle, stoppered by a thumb.

"Yay, Penrod!" the visitor gave greeting.

"Yay," said Penrod with slight enthusiasm. "What you got?"

"Lickrish water."

"Drinkin's!" demanded Penrod promptly. This is equivalent to the cry of "Biters" when an apple is shown, and establishes unquestionable title.

"Down to there!" stipulated Sam, removing his thumb to affix it firmly as a mark upon the side of the bottle — a check upon gormandizing that remained carefully in place while Penrod drank. This rite concluded, the visitor's eye fell upon the basket deposited by Della. He emitted tokens of pleasure.

"Looky! Looky! Looky there! That ain't any good pile o' stuff — oh, no!"

"What for?"

"Drug store!" shouted Sam. "We'll be partners ——"

"Or else," Penrod suggested, "I'll run the drug store and you be a customer ——"

"No! Partners!" insisted Sam with such con-

viction that his host yielded; and within ten minutes
the drug store was doing a heavy business with imaginary patrons.   Improvising counters with boards
and boxes, and setting forth a very druggish-looking
stock from the basket, each of the partners found
occupation to his taste — Penrod as salesman and
Sam as prescription clerk.

"Here you are, madam!" said Penrod briskly,
offering a vial of Sam's mixing to an invisible matron.
"This will cure your husband in a few minutes.
Here's the camphor, mister. Call again! Fifty
cents' worth of pills? Yes, madam. There you are!
Hurry up with that dose for the nigger lady,
Bill!"

"I'll tend to it soon's I get time, Jim," replied the
prescription clerk.   "I'm busy fixin' the smallpox
medicine for the sick policeman downtown."

Penrod stopped sales to watch this operation.
Sam had found an empty pint bottle and, with the
pursed lips and measuring eye of a great chemist, was
engaged in filling it from other bottles. First, he
poured into it some of the syrup from the condemned
preserves; and a quantity of extinct hair oil; next the
remaining contents of a dozen small vials cryptically
labelled with physicians' prescriptions; then some

Penrod stopped sales to watch this operation

remnants of catsup and essence of beef and what was left in several bottles of mouthwash; after that a quantity of rejected flavouring extract — topping off by shaking into the mouth of the bottle various powders from small pink papers, relics of Mr. Schofield's influenza of the preceding winter.

Sam examined the combination with concern, appearing unsatisfied. "We got to make that smallpox medicine good and strong!" he remarked; and, his artistic sense growing more powerful than his appetite, he poured about a quarter of the licorice water into the smallpox medicine.

"What you doin'?" protested Penrod. "What you want to waste that lickrish water for? We ought to keep it to drink when we're tired."

"I guess I got a right to use my own lickrish water any way I want to," replied the prescription clerk. "I tell you, you can't get smallpox medicine too strong. Look at her now!" He held the bottle up admiringly. "She's as black as lickrish. I bet you she's strong all right!"

"I wonder how she tastes?" said Penrod thoughtfully.

"Don't smell so awful much," observed Sam, sniffing the bottle — "a good deal, though!"

"I wonder if it'd make us sick to drink it?" said Penrod.

Sam looked at the bottle thoughtfully; then his eye, wandering, fell upon Duke, placidly curled up near the door, and lighted with the advent of an idea new to him, but old, old in the world — older than Egypt!

"Let's give Duke some!" he cried.

That was the spark. They acted immediately; and a minute later Duke, released from custody with a competent potion of the smallpox medicine inside him, settled conclusively their doubts concerning its effect. The patient animal, accustomed to expect the worst at all times, walked out of the door, shaking his head with an air of considerable annoyance, opening and closing his mouth with singular energy — and so repeatedly that they began to count the number of times he did it. Sam thought it was thirty-nine times, but Penrod had counted forty-one before other and more striking symptoms appeared.

All things come from Mother Earth and must return — Duke restored much at this time. Afterward, he ate heartily of grass; and then, over his shoulder, he bent upon his master one inscrutable look and departed feebly to the front yard.

The two boys had watched the process with warm interest. "I told you she was strong!" said Mr. Williams proudly.

"Yes, sir — she is!" Penrod was generous enough to admit. "I expect she's strong enough ——" He paused in thought, and added: "We haven't got a horse any more."

"I bet you she'd fix him if you had!" said Sam. And it may be that this was no idle boast.

The pharmaceutical game was not resumed; the experiment upon Duke had made the drug store commonplace and stimulated the appetite for stronger meat. Lounging in the doorway, the near-vivisectionists sipped licorice water alternately and conversed.

"I bet some of our smallpox medicine would fix ole P'fessor Bartet all right!" quoth Penrod. "I wish he'd come along and ask us for some."

"We could tell him it was lickrish water," added Sam, liking the idea. "The two bottles look almost the same."

"Then we wouldn't have to go to his ole cotillon this afternoon," Penrod sighed. "There wouldn't be any!"

"Who's your partner, Pen?"

"Who's yours?"

"Who's yours? I just ast you."

"Oh, she's all right!" And Penrod smiled boastfully.

"I bet you wanted to dance with Marjorie!" said his friend.

"Me? I wouldn't dance with that girl if she begged me to! I wouldn't dance with her to save her from drowning! I wouldn't da ——"

"Oh, no — you wouldn't!" interrupted Mr. Williams skeptically.

Penrod changed his tone and became persuasive.

"Looky here, Sam," he said confidentially. "I've got a mighty nice partner, but my mother don't like her mother; and so I've been thinking I better not dance with her. I'll tell you what I'll do; I've got a mighty good sling in the house, and I'll give it to you if you'll change partners."

"You want to change and you don't even know who mine is!" said Sam, and he made the simple though precocious deduction: "Yours must be a lala! Well, I invited Mabel Rorebeck, and she wouldn't let me change if I wanted to. Mabel Rorebeck'd rather dance with me," he continued serenely, "than anybody; and she said she was awful

afraid you'd ast her.   But I ain't goin' to dance with
Mabel after all, because this morning she sent me a
note about her uncle died last night — and P'fessor Bartet'll have to find me a partner after I get
there.   Anyway I bet you haven't got any sling —
and I bet your partner's Baby Rennsdale!"

"What if she is?" said Penrod.   "She's good
enough for *me!*" This speech held not so much
modesty in solution as intended praise of the lady.
Taken literally, however, it was an understatement
of the facts and wholly insincere.

"Yay!" jeered Mr. Williams, upon whom his
friend's hypocrisy was quite wasted.   "How can
your mother not like her mother?   Baby Rennsdale
hasn't got any mother!   You and her'll be a sight!"

That was Penrod's own conviction; and with this
corroboration of it he grew so spiritless that he could
offer no retort.   He slid to a despondent sitting posture upon the doorsill and gazed wretchedly upon
the ground, while his companion went to replenish
the licorice water at the hydrant — enfeebling the
potency of the liquor no doubt, but making up for
that in quantity.

"Your mother goin' with you to the cotillon?"
asked Sam when he returned.

"No. She's goin' to meet me there. She's goin' somewhere first."

"So's mine," said Sam. "I'll come by for you."

"All right."

"I better go before long. Noon whistles been blowin'."

"All right, " Penrod repeated dully.

Sam turned to go, but paused. A new straw hat was peregrinating along the fence near the two boys. This hat belonged to some one passing upon the sidewalk of the cross-street; and the some one was Maurice Levy. Even as they stared, he halted and regarded them over the fence with two small, dark eyes.

Fate had brought about this moment and this confrontation.

CHAPTER XIV

MAURICE LEVY'S CONSTITUTION

"LO, SAM!" said Maurice cautiously. "What you doin'?"

Penrod at that instant had a singular experience — an intellectual shock like a flash of fire in the brain. Sitting in darkness, a great light flooded him with wild brilliance. He gasped!

"What you doin'?" repeated Mr. Levy.

Penrod sprang to his feet, seized the licorice bottle, shook it with stoppering thumb, and took a long drink with histrionic unction.

"What you doin'?" asked Maurice for the third time, Sam Williams not having decided upon a reply.

It was Penrod who answered.

"Drinkin' lickrish water," he said simply, and wiped his mouth with such delicious enjoyment that Sam's jaded thirst was instantly stimulated. He took the bottle eagerly from Penrod.

"A-a-h!" exclaimed Penrod, smacking his lips. "That was a good un!"

The eyes above the fence glistened.

"Ask him if he don't want some," Penrod whispered urgently. "Quit drinkin' it! It's no good any more. Ask him!"

"What for?" demanded the practical Sam.

"Go on and ask him!" whispered Penrod fiercely.

"Say, M'rice!" Sam called, waving the bottle. "Want some?"

"Bring it here!" Mr. Levy requested.

"Come on over and get some," returned Sam, being prompted.

"I can't. Penrod Schofield's after me."

"No, I'm not," said Penrod reassuringly. "I won't touch you, M'rice. I made up with you yesterday afternoon — don't you remember? You're all right with me, M'rice."

Maurice looked undecided. But Penrod had the delectable bottle again, and tilting it above his lips, affected to let the cool liquid purl enrichingly into him, while with his right hand he stroked his middle facade ineffably. Maurice's mouth watered.

"Here!" cried Sam, stirred again by the superb manifestations of his friend. "Gimme that!"

Penrod brought the bottle down, surprisingly full after so much gusto, but withheld it from Sam; and the two scuffled for its possession. Nothing in the world could have so worked upon the desire of the yearning observer beyond the fence.

"Honest, Penrod — you ain't goin' to touch me if I come in your yard?" he called. "Honest?"

"Cross my heart!" answered Penrod, holding the bottle away from Sam. "And we'll let you drink all you want."

Maurice hastily climbed the fence, and while he was thus occupied Mr. Samuel Williams received a great enlightenment. With startling rapidity Penrod, standing just outside the storeroom door, extended his arm within the room, deposited the licorice water upon the counter of the drug store, seized in its stead the bottle of smallpox medicine, and extended it cordially toward the advancing Maurice.

Genius is like that — great, simple, broad strokes!

Dazzled, Mr. Samuel Williams leaned against the wall. He had the sensations of one who comes suddenly into the presence of a chef-d'œuvre. Perhaps his first coherent thought was that almost universal one on such huge occasions: "Why couldn't *I* have done that!"

Sam might have been even more dazzled had he guessed that he figured not altogether as a spectator in the sweeping and magnificent conception of the new Talleyrand. Sam had no partner for the cotillon. If Maurice was to be absent from that festivity — as it began to seem he might be — Penrod needed a male friend to take care of Miss Rennsdale; and he believed he saw his way to compel Mr. Williams to be that male friend. For this he relied largely upon the prospective conduct of Miss Rennsdale when he should get the matter before her — he was inclined to believe she would favour the exchange. As for Talleyrand Penrod himself, he was going to dance that cotillon with Marjorie Jones!

"You can have all you can drink at one pull, M'rice," said Penrod kindly.

"You said I could have all I want!" protested Maurice, reaching for the bottle.

"No, I didn't," returned Penrod quickly, holding it away from the eager hand.

"He did, too! Didn't he, Sam?"

Sam could not reply; his eyes, fixed upon the bottle, protruded strangely.

"You heard him — didn't you, Sam?"

"Well, if I did say it I didn't mean it!" said Penrod hastily, quoting from one of the authorities. "Looky here, M'rice," he continued, assuming a more placative and reasoning tone, "that wouldn't be fair to us. I guess we want some of our own lickrish water, don't we? The bottle ain't much over two-thirds full anyway. What I meant was, you can have all you can drink at one pull."

"How do you mean?"

"Why, this way: you can gulp all you want, so long as you keep swallering; but you can't take the bottle out of your mouth and commence again. Soon's you quit swallering it's Sam's turn."

"No; you can have next, Penrod," said Sam.

"Well, anyway, I mean M'rice has to give the bottle up the minute he stops swallering."

Craft appeared upon the face of Maurice, like a poster pasted on a wall.

"I can drink so long I don't stop swallering?"

"Yes; that's it."

"All right!" he cried.   "Gimme the bottle!"

And Penrod placed it in his hand.

"You promise to let me drink until I quit swallering?" Maurice insisted.

"Yes!" said both boys together.

With that, Maurice placed the bottle to his lips and began to drink.   Penrod and Sam leaned forward in breathless excitement.   They had feared Maurice might smell the contents of the bottle; but that danger was past — this was the crucial moment. Their fondest hope was that he would make his first swallow a voracious one — it was impossible to imagine a second.   They expected one big, gulping swallow and then an explosion, with fountain effects.

Little they knew the mettle of their man!   Maurice swallowed once; he swallowed twice — and thrice   and he continued to swallow!   No Adam's apple was sculptured on that juvenile throat, but the internal progress of the liquid was not a whit the less visible.   His eyes gleamed with cunning and malicious triumph, sidewise, at the stunned conspirators; he was fulfilling the conditions of the draught, not once breaking the thread of that marvellous swallering.

His audience stood petrified. Already Maurice had swallowed more than they had given Duke — and still the liquor receded in the uplifted bottle! And now the clear glass gleamed above the dark contents full half the vessel's length — and Maurice went on drinking! Slowly the clear glass increased in its dimensions — slowly the dark diminished.

Sam Williams made a horrified movement to check him — but Maurice protested passionately with his disengaged arm, and made vehement vocal noises remindful of the contract; whereupon Sam desisted and watched the continuing performance in a state of grisly fascination.

Maurice drank it all! He drained the last drop and threw the bottle in the air, uttering loud ejaculations of triumph and satisfaction.

"Hah!" he cried, blowing out his cheeks, inflating his chest, squaring his shoulders, patting his stomach, and wiping his mouth contentedly. "Hah! Aha! Waha! Wafwah! But that was good!"

The two boys stood looking at him in a stupor.

"Well, I gotta say this," said Maurice graciously: "You stuck to your bargain all right and treated me fair."

Stricken with a sudden horrible suspicion, Penrod

entered the storeroom in one stride and lifted the bottle of licorice water to his nose — then to his lips. It was weak, but good; he had made no mistake. And Maurice had really drained — to the dregs — the bottle of old hair tonics, dead catsups, syrups of undesirable preserves, condemned extracts of vanilla and lemon, decayed chocolate, exessence of beef, mixed dental preparations, aromatic spirits of ammonia, spirits of nitre, alcohol, arnica, quinine, ipecac, sal volatile, nux vomica and licorice water — with traces of arsenic, belladonna and strychnine.

Penrod put the licorice water out of sight and turned to face the others. Maurice was seating himself on a box just outside the door and had taken a package of cigarettes from his pocket.

"Nobody can see me from here, can they?" he said, striking a match. "You fellers smoke?"

"No," said Sam, staring at him haggardly.

"No," said Penrod in a whisper.

Maurice lit his cigarette and puffed showily.

"Well, sir," he remarked, "you fellers are certainly square — I gotta say that much. Honest, Penrod, I thought you was after me! I did think so," he added sunnily; "but now I guess you like

me, or else you wouldn't of stuck to it about lettin'
me drink it all if I kept on swallering."

He chatted on with complete geniality, smoking
his cigarette in content. And as he ran from one
topic to another his hearers stared at him in a kind
of torpor. Never once did they exchange a glance
with each other; their eyes were frozen to Maurice.
The cheerful conversationalist made it evident that
he was not without gratitude.

"Well," he said as he finished his cigarette and
rose to go, " you fellers have treated me nice — and
some day you come over to my yard; I'd like to
run with you fellers. You're the kind of fellers I
like."

Penrod's jaw fell; Sam's mouth had been open all
the time. Neither spoke.

"I gotta go," observed Maurice, consulting a
handsome watch. "Gotta get dressed for the cotillon right after lunch. Come on, Sam. Don't
you have to go, too?"

Sam nodded dazedly.

"Well, good-bye, Penrod," said Maurice cordially. "I'm glad you like me all right. Come on,
Sam."

Penrod leaned against the doorpost and with fixed

and glazing eyes watched the departure of his two visitors. Maurice was talking volubly, with much gesticulation, as they went; but Sam walked mechanically and in silence, staring at his brisk companion and keeping at a little distance from him.

They passed from sight, Maurice still conversing gayly — and Penrod slowly betook himself into the house, his head bowed upon his chest.

Some three hours later, Mr. Samuel Williams, waxen clean and in sweet raiment, made his reappearance in Penrod's yard, yodelling a code-signal to summon forth his friend. He yodelled loud, long, and frequently, finally securing a faint response from the upper air.

"Where are you?" shouted Mr. Williams, his roving glance searching ambient heights. Another low-spirited yodel reaching his ear, he perceived the head and shoulders of his friend projecting above the roofridge of the stable. The rest of Penrod's body was concealed from view, reposing upon the opposite slant of the gable and precariously secured by the crooking of his elbows over the ridge.

"Yay! What you doin' up there?"

"Nothin'."

"You better be careful!" Sam called. "You'll slide off and fall down in the alley if you don't look out. I come pert' near it last time we was up there. Come on down! Ain't you goin' to the cotillon?"

Penrod made no reply. Sam came nearer.

"Say," he called up in a guarded voice, "I went to our telephone a while ago and ast him how he was feelin', and he said he felt fine!"

"So did I," said Penrod. "He told me he felt bully!"

Sam thrust his hands in his pockets and brooded. The opening of the kitchen door caused a diversion. It was Della.

"Mister Penrod," she bellowed forthwith, "come ahn down fr'm up there! Y'r mamma's at the dancin' class waitin' fer ye, an' she's telephoned me they're goin' to begin — an' what's the matter with ye? Come ahn down fr'm up there!"

"Come on!" urged Sam. "We'll be late. There go Maurice and Marjorie now."

A glittering car spun by, disclosing briefly a genre picture of Marjorie Jones in pink, supporting a monstrous sheaf of American Beauty roses. Maurice, sitting shining and joyous beside her, saw both boys.

and waved them a hearty greeting as the car turned the corner.

Penrod uttered some muffled words and then waved both arms — either in response or as an expression of his condition of mind; it may have been a gesture of despair. How much intention there was in this act — obviously so rash, considering the position he occupied — it is impossible to say. Undeniably there must remain a suspicion of deliberate purpose.

Della screamed and Sam shouted. Penrod had disappeared from view.

The delayed dancing class was about to begin a most uneven cotillon under the direction of its slightly frenzied instructor, when Samuel Williams arrived.

Mrs. Schofield hurriedly left the ballroom; while Miss Rennsdale, flushing with sudden happiness, curtsied profoundly to Professor Bartet and obtained his attention.

"I have told you fifty times," he informed her passionately erc she spoke, "I cannot make no such changes. If your partner comes you have to dance with him. You are going to drive me crazy, sure! What is it? What now? What you want?"

The damsel curtsied again and handed him the following communication, addressed to herself:

"Dear madam Please excuse me from dancing the cotilon with you this afternoon as I have fell off the barn

"Sincerly yours

"PENROD SCHOFIELD."

CHAPTER XV

THE TWO FAMILIES

PENROD entered the schoolroom, Monday morning, picturesquely leaning upon a man's cane shortened to support a cripple approaching the age of twelve. He arrived about twenty minutes late, limping deeply, his brave young mouth drawn with pain, and the sensation he created must have been a solace to him; the only possible criticism of this entrance being that it was just a shade too heroic. Perhaps for that reason it failed to stagger Miss Spence, a woman so saturated with suspicion that she penalized Penrod for tardiness as promptly and as coldly as if he had been a mere, ordinary, unmutilated boy. Nor would she entertain any discussion of the justice of her ruling. It seemed, almost, that she feared to argue with him.

However, the distinction of cane and limp remained to him, consolations which he protracted far into the week — until Thursday evening, in fact, when Mr. Schofield, observing from a window his son's pursuit of Duke round and round the backyard, confiscated the cane, with the promise that it should not remain idle if he saw Penrod limping again. Thus, succeeding a depressing Friday, another Saturday brought the necessity for new inventions.

It was a scented morning in apple-blossom time. At about ten of the clock Penrod emerged hastily from the kitchen door. His pockets bulged abnormally; so did his cheeks, and he swallowed with difficulty. A threatening mop, wielded by a cooklike arm in a checkered sleeve, followed him through the doorway, and he was preceded by a small, hurried, wistful dog with a warm doughnut in his mouth. The kitchen door slammed petulantly, enclosing the sore voice of Della, whereupon Penrod and Duke seated themselves upon the pleasant sward and immediately consumed the spoils of their raid.

At about ten of the clock Penrod emerged hastily from the kitchen door

145

From the cross-street which formed the side boundary of the Schofields' ample yard came a jingle of harness and the cadenced clatter of a pair of trotting horses, and Penrod, looking up, beheld the passing of a fat acquaintance, torpid amid the conservative splendours of a rather old-fashioned victoria. This was Roderick Magsworth Bitts, Junior, a fellow sufferer at the Friday Afternoon Dancing Class, but otherwise not often a companion; a home-sheltered lad, tutored privately and preserved against the coarsening influences of rude comradeship and miscellaneous information. Heavily overgrown in all physical dimensions, virtuous, and placid, this cloistered mutton was wholly uninteresting to Penrod Schofield. Nevertheless, Roderick Magsworth Bitts, Junior, was a personage on account of the importance of the Magsworth Bitts family; and it was Penrod's destiny to increase Roderick's celebrity far, far beyond its present aristocratic limitations.

The Magsworth Bittses were important because they were impressive; there was no other reason. And they were impressive because they believed themselves important. The adults of the family were impregnably formal; they dressed with reticent elegance, and wore the same nose and the same expression — an expression which indicated that they knew something exquisite and sacred which other people could never know. Other people, in their presence, were apt to feel mysteriously ignoble and to become secretly uneasy about ancestors, gloves, and pronunciation. The Magsworth Bitts manner was withholding and reserved, though sometimes gracious, granting small smiles as great favours and giving off a chilling kind of preciousness. Naturally, when any citizen of the community did anything unconventional or improper, or made a mistake, or had a relative who went wrong, that citizen's first and worst fear was that the Magsworth Bittses would hear of it. In fact, this painful family had for years terrorized the community, though the community had never realized that it was terrorized, and invariably spoke of the family as the "most charming circle in town." By common consent, Mrs. Roderick Magsworth Bitts officiated as the supreme model as well as critic-in-chief of morals and deportment for all the unlucky people prosperous enough to be elevated to her acquaintance.

Magsworth was the important part of the name. Mrs. Roderick Magsworth Bitts was a Magsworth

born, herself, and the Magsworth crest decorated
not only Mrs. Magsworth Bitts' note-paper but
was on the china, on the table linen, on the chimney-
pieces, on the opaque glass of the front door, on the
victoria, and on the harness, though omitted from
the garden-hose and the lawn-mower.

Naturally, no sensible person dreamed of connecting that illustrious crest with the unfortunate
and notorious Rena Magsworth whose name had
grown week by week into larger and larger type upon
the front pages of newspapers, owing to the gradually increasing public and official belief that she
had poisoned a family of eight. However, the statement that no sensible person could have connected
the Magsworth Bitts family with the arsenical Rena
takes no account of Penrod Schofield.

Penrod never missed a murder, a hanging or an
electrocution in the newspapers; he knew almost as
much about Rena Magsworth as her jurymen did,
though they sat in a court-room two hundred miles
away, and he had it in mind — so frank he was —
to ask Roderick Magsworth Bitts, Junior, if the
murderess happened to be a relative.

The present encounter, being merely one of apa-
thetic greeting, did not afford the opportunity. Pen-

rod took off his cap, and Roderick, seated between his mother and one of his grown-up sisters, nodded sluggishly, but neither Mrs. Magsworth Bitts nor her daughter acknowledged the salutation of the boy in the yard. They disapproved of him as a person of little consequence, and that little, bad. Snubbed, Penrod thoughtfully restored his cap to his head. A boy can be cut as effectually as a man, and this one was chilled to a low temperature. He wondered if they despised him because they had seen a last fragment of doughnut in his hand; then he thought that perhaps it was Duke who had disgraced him. Duke was certainly no fashionable looking dog.

The resilient spirits of youth, however, presently revived, and discovering a spider upon one knee and a beetle simultaneously upon the other, Penrod forgot Mrs. Roderick Magsworth Bitts in the course of some experiments infringing upon the domain of Doctor Carrel. Penrod's efforts — with the aid of a pin — to effect a transference of living organism were unsuccessful; but he convinced himself forever that a spider cannot walk with a beetle's legs. Della then enhanced zoölogical interest by depositing upon the back porch a large rat-trap from the cellar, the prison of four live rats awaiting execution.

Penrod at once took possession, retiring to the empty stable, where he installed the rats in a small wooden box with a sheet of broken window-glass — held down by a brickbat — over the top. Thus the symptoms of their agitation, when the box was shaken or hammered upon, could be studied at leisure. Altogether this Saturday was starting splendidly.

After a time, the student's attention was withdrawn from his specimens by a peculiar smell, which, being followed up by a system of selective sniffing, proved to be an emanation leaking into the stable from the alley. He opened the back door.

Across the alley was a cottage which a thrifty neighbour had built on the rear line of his lot and rented to negroes; and the fact that a negro family was now in process of "moving in" was manifested by the presence of a thin mule and a ramshackle wagon, the latter laden with the semblance of a stove and a few other unpretentious household articles.

A very small darky boy stood near the mule. In his hand was a rusty chain, and at the end of the chain the delighted Penrod perceived the source of the special smell he was tracing — a large raccoon.

Duke, who had shown not the slightest interest in the rats, set up a frantic barking and simulated a ravening assault upon the strange animal. It was only a bit of acting, however, for Duke was an old dog, had suffered much, and desired no unnecessary sorrow, wherefore he confined his demonstrations to alarums and excursions, and presently sat down at a distance and expressed himself by intermittent threatenings in a quavering falsetto.

"What's that 'coon's name?" asked Penrod, intending no discourtesy.

"Aim gommo mame," said the small darky.

"What?"

"Aim gommo mame."

"*What?*"

The small darky looked annoyed.

"Aim *gommo* mame, I hell you," he said impatiently.

Penrod conceived that insult was intended.

"What's the matter of you?" he demanded advancing. "You get fresh with *me*, and I'll ——"

"Hyuh, white boy!" A coloured youth of Penrod's own age appeared in the doorway of the cottage. "You let 'at brothuh mine alone. He ain' do nothin' to you."

"Well, why can't he answer?"

"He can't. He can't talk no better'n what he *was* talkin'. He tongue-tie'."

"Oh," said Penrod, mollified. Then, obeying an impulse so universally aroused in the human breast under like circumstances that it has become a quip, he turned to the afflicted one.

"Talk some more," he begged eagerly.

"I hoe you ackoom aim gommo mame," was the prompt response, in which a slight ostentation was manifest. Unmistakable tokens of vanity had appeared upon the small, swart countenance.

"What's he mean?" asked Penrod, enchanted.

"He say he tole you 'at 'coon ain' got no name."

"What's *your* name?"

"I'm name Herman."

"What's his name?" Penrod pointed to the tongue-tied boy.

"Verman."

"What!"

"Verman. Was three us boys in ow fam'ly. Ol'est one name Sherman. 'N 'en come me; I'm Herman. 'N 'en come him; he Verman. Sherman dead. Verman, he de littles' one."

"You goin' to live here?"

"Umhuh. Done move in f'm way outen on a fahm."

He pointed to the north with his right hand, and Penrod's eyes opened wide as they followed the gesture. Herman had no forefinger on that hand.

"Look there!" exclaimed Penrod. "You haven't got any finger!"

"*I* mum map," said Verman, with egregious pride.

"*He* done 'at," interpreted Herman, chuckling. "Yessuh; done chop 'er spang off, long 'go. He's a playin' wif a ax an' I lay my finguh on de do'-sill an' I say, 'Verman, chop 'er off!' So Verman he chop 'er right spang off up to de roots! Yessuh."

"What *for?*"

"Jes' fo' nothin'."

"He hoe me hoo," remarked Verman.

"Yessuh, I tole him to," said Herman, "an' he chop 'er off, an' ey ain't airy oth' one evuh grow on wheres de ole one use to grow. Nosuh!"

"But what'd you tell him to do it for?"

"Nothin'. I jes' said it 'at way — an' he jes' chop 'er off!"

Both brothers looked pleased and proud. Penrod's profound interest was flatteringly visible, a tribute to their unusualness.

"Hem bow goy," suggested Verman eagerly.

"Aw ri'," said Herman. "Ow sistuh Queenie, she a growed-up woman; she got a goituh."

"Got a what?"

"Goituh. Swellin' on her neck — grea' big swellin'. She heppin' mammy move in now. You look in de front-room winduh wheres she sweepin'; you kin see it on her."

Penrod looked in the window and was rewarded by a fine view of Queenie's goitre. He had never before seen one, and only the lure of further conversation on the part of Verman brought him from the window.

"Verman say tell you 'bout pappy," explained Herman. "Mammy an' Queenie move in town an' go git de house all fix up befo' pappy git out."

"Out of where?"

"Jail. Pappy cut a man, an' de police done kep' him in jail evuh sense Chris'mus-time; but dey goin' tuhn him loose ag'in nex' week."

"What'd he cut the other man with?"

"Wif a pitchfawk."

Penrod began to feel that a lifetime spent with this fascinating family were all too short. The brothers, glowing with amiability, were as enraptured as he. For the first time in their lives they moved in the rich glamour of sensationalism. Herman was prodigal of gesture with his right hand; and Verman, chuckling with delight, talked fluently, though somewhat consciously. They cheerfully agreed to keep the raccoon — already beginning to be mentioned as "our 'coon" by Penrod — in Mr. Schofield's empty stable, and, when the animal had been chained to the wall near the box of rats and supplied with a pan of fair water, they assented to their new friend's suggestion (inspired by a fine sense of the artistic harmonies) that the heretofore nameless pet be christened Sherman, in honour of their deceased relative.

At this juncture was heard from the front yard the sound of that yodelling which is the peculiar accomplishment of those whose voices have not "changed." Penrod yodelled a response; and Mr. Samuel Williams appeared, a large bundle under his arm.

"Yay, Penrod!" was his greeting, casual enough from without; but, having entered, he stopped short and emitted a prodigious whistle. "*Ya-a-ay!*" he then shouted. "Look at the 'coon!"

"I guess you better say, 'Look at the 'coon!'" Penrod returned proudly. "They's a good deal

more'n him to look at, too. Talk some, Verman."
Verman complied.

Sam was warmly interested. "What'd you say
his name was?" he asked.

"Verman."

"How d'you spell it?"

"V-e-r-m-a-n," replied Penrod, having previously
received this information from Herman.

"Oh!" said Sam.

"Point to sumpthing, Herman," Penrod commanded, and Sam's excitement, when Herman
pointed was sufficient to the occasion.

Penrod, the discoverer, continued his exploitation
of the manifold wonders of the Sherman, Herman,
and Verman collection. With the air of a proprietor
he escorted Sam into the alley for a good look at
Queenie (who seemed not to care for her increasing
celebrity) and proceeded to a dramatic climax —
the recital of the episode of the pitchfork and its
consequences.

The cumulative effect was enormous, and could
have but one possible result. The normal boy is
always at least one half Barnum.

"Let's get up a SHOW!"

Penrod and Sam both claimed to have said it

first, a question left unsettled in the ecstasies of hurried preparation. The bundle under Sam's arm, brought with no definite purpose, proved to have been an inspiration. It consisted of broad sheets of light yellow wrapping-paper, discarded by Sam's mother in her spring house-cleaning. There were half-filled cans and buckets of paint in the storeroom adjoining the carriage-house, and presently the side wall of the stable flamed information upon the passer-by from a great and spreading poster.

"Publicity," primal requisite of all theatrical and amphitheatrical enterprise thus provided, subsequent arrangements proceeded with a fury of energy which transformed the empty hay-loft. True, it is impossible to say just what the hay-loft was transformed into, but history warrantably clings to the statement that it was transformed. Duke and Sherman were secured to the rear wall at a considerable distance from each other, after an exhibition of reluctance on the part of Duke, during which he displayed a nervous energy and agility almost miraculous in so small and middle-aged a dog. Benches were improvised for spectators; the rats were brought up; finally the rafters, corn-crib, and hay-chute were ornamented with flags and strips of bunting from

Sam Williams' attic, Sam returning from the excursion wearing an old silk hat, and accompanied (on account of a rope) by a fine dachshund encountered on the highway. In the matter of personal decoration paint was generously used: an interpretation of the spiral, inclining to whites and greens, becoming brilliantly effective upon the dark facial backgrounds of Herman and Verman; while the countenances of Sam and Penrod were each supplied with the black moustache and imperial, lacking which, no professional showman can be esteemed conscientious.

It was regretfully decided, in council, that no attempt be made to add Queenie to the list of exhibits, her brothers warmly declining to act as ambassadors in that cause. They were certain Queenie would not like the idea, they said, and Herman picturesquely described her activity on occasions when she had been annoyed by too much attention to her appearance. However, Penrod's disappointment was alleviated by an inspiration which came to him in a moment of pondering upon the dachshund, and the entire party went forth to add an enriching line to the poster.

They found a group of seven, including two adults,

already gathered in the street to read and ad**mire** this work.

SCHoFiELD & WiLLiAMS
BiG SHOW
ADMiSSioN 1 CENT oR 20 PiNS
MUSUEM oF CURioSiTES
Now GoiNG oN
SHERMAN HERMAN & VERMAN
THiER FATHERS iN JAiL STABED A
MAN WiTH A
PiTCHFORK
SHERMAN THE WiLD ANIMAL
CAPTURED iN AFRiCA
HERMAN THE ONE FiNGEREĎ TATOOD
WILD MAN VERMAN THE SAVAGE TATOOD
WILD BoY TALKS ONLY iN HiS NAiTiVE
LANGUAGS. Do NoT FAIL TO SEE DUKE
THE INDiAN DOG ALSO THE MiCHiGAN
TRAiNED RATS

A heated argument took place between Sam and Penrod, the point at issue being settled, finally, by the drawing of straws; whereupon Penrod, with pardonable self-importance — in the presence of an audience now increased to nine — slowly painted the words inspired by the dachshund:

IMPoRTENT Do NoT MISS THE SoUTH AMERiCAN DoG PART ALLIGATOR.

CHAPTER XVI

THE NEW STAR

SAM, Penrod, Herman, and Verman withdrew in considerable state from non-paying view, and, repairing to the hay-loft, declared the exhibition open to the public. Oral proclamation was made by Sam, and then the loitering multitude was enticed by the seductive strains of a band; the two partners performing upon combs and paper, Herman and Verman upon tin pans with sticks.

The effect was immediate. Visitors appeared upon the stairway and sought admission. Herman and Verman took position among the exhibits, near the wall; Sam stood at the entrance, officiating as barker and ticket-seller; while Penrod, with debonair suavity, acted as curator, master of ceremonies, and lecturer.   He greeted the first to enter with a courtly bow. They consisted of Miss Rennsdale and her nursery governess, and they paid spot cash for their admission.

"Walk in, lay-deeze, walk right in — pray do not ob- struck the passageway," said Penrod, in a remarkable voice. "Pray be seated; there is room for each and all."

Miss Rennsdale and governess were followed by Mr. Georgie Bassett and baby sister (which proves the perfection of Georgie's character) and six or seven other neighbourhood children — a most satisfactory audience, although, subsequent to Miss Rennsdale and governess, admission was wholly by pin.

"*Gen*-til-mun and *lay*-deeze," shouted Penrod, "I will first call your at-tain-shon to our genuine South American dog, part alligator!" He pointed to the dachshund, and added, in his ordinary tone, "That's him." Straightway reassuming the char- acter of showman, he bellowed: "*Next*, you see Duke, the genuine, full-blooded Indian dog from the Far Western Plains and Rocky Mountains. *Next*, the trained Michigan rats, captured way up there, and trained to jump and run all around the box at the — at the — at the slightest *pre*-text!" He paused, partly to take breath and partly to enjoy his own surprised discovery that this phrase was in his vocabulary.

"At the slightest *pre*-text!" he repeated, and continued, suiting the action to the word: " I will now hammer upon the box and each and all may see these genuine full-blooded Michigan rats perform at the slightest *pre*-text! There! (That's all they do now, but I and Sam are goin' to train 'em lots more before this afternoon.) *Gen*-til-mun and *lay*-deeze, I will kindly now call your at-tain-shon to Sherman, the wild animal from Africa, costing the lives of the wild trapper and many of his companions. *Next*, let me kindly interodoos Herman and Verman. Their father got mad and stuck his pitchfork right inside of another man, exactly as promised upon the advertisements outside the big tent, and got put in jail. Look at them well, gen-til-mun and lay-deeze, there is no extra charge, and *re-mem-bur* you are each and all now looking at two wild, tattooed men which the father of is in jail. Point, Herman. Each and all will have a chance to see. Point to sumpthing else, Herman. This is the only genuine

one-fingered tattooed wild man. Last on the pro-
gramme, gen-til-mun and lay-deeze, we have Verman,
the savage tattooed wild boy, that can't speak only
his native foreign languages. Talk some, Verman."

Verman obliged and made an instantaneous hit.
He was encored rapturously, again and again; and,
thrilling with the unique pleasure of being appreciated
and misunderstood at the same time, would have
talked all day but too gladly. Sam Williams, however, with a true showman's foresight, whispered
to Penrod, who rang down on the monologue.

"*Gen*-til-mun and *lay*-deeze, this closes our pufformance. Pray pass out quietly and with as little
jostling as possible. As soon as you are all out
there's goin' to be a new pufformance, and each and
all are welcome at the same and simple price of admission. Pray pass out quietly and with as little
jostling as possible. *Re-mem-bur* the price is only
one cent, the tenth part of a dime, or twenty pins,
no bent ones taken. Pray pass out quietly and with
as little jostling as possible. The Schofield and
Williams Military Band will play before each pufformance, and each and all are welcome for the same
and simple price of admission. Pray pass out quietly
and with as little jostling as possible."

Forthwith, the Schofield and Williams Military Band began a second overture, in which something vaguely like a tune was at times distinguishable; and all of the first audience returned, most of them having occupied the interval in hasty excursions for more pins; Miss Rennsdale and governess, however, again paying coin of the Republic and receiving deference and the best seats accordingly. And when a third performance found all of the same in-veterate patrons once more crowding the auditorium, and seven recruits added, the pleasurable excitement of the partners in their venture will be understood by any one who has seen a metropolitan manager strolling about the foyer of his theatre some even-ing during the earlier stages of an assured "phe-nomenal run."

From the first, there was no question which feature of the entertainment was the attraction extraordi-nary: Verman — Verman, the savage tattooed wild boy, speaking only his native foreign languages — Verman was a triumph! Beaming, wreathed in smiles, melodious, incredibly fluent, he had but to open his lips and a dead hush fell upon the audience. Breathless, they leaned forward, hanging upon his every semi-syllable, and, when Penrod checked the flow, burst into thunders of applause, which Verman received with happy laughter.

Alas! he delayed not o'er long to display all the egregiousness of a new star; but for a time there was no caprice of his too eccentric to be forgiven. During Penrod's lecture upon the other curios, the tattooed wild boy continually stamped his foot, grinned, and gesticulated, tapping his tiny chest, and pointing to himself as it were to say: "Wait for Me! *I* am the Big Show." So soon they learn; so soon they learn! And (again alas!) this spoiled darling of public favour, like many another, was fated to know, in good time, the fickleness of that favour.

But during all the morning performances he was the idol of his audience and looked it! The climax of his popularity came during the fifth overture of the Schofield and Williams Military Band, when the music was quite drowned in the agitated clamours of Miss Rennsdale, who was endeavouring to ascend the stairs in spite of the physical dissuasion of her governess.

"I *won't* go home to lunch!" screamed Miss Rennsdale, her voice accompanied by a sound of ripping. "I *will* hear the tattooed wild boy talk some more! It's lovely — I *will* hear him talk! I *will!* I *will!*

Maurice Levy appeared, escorting Marjorie Jones, and paid coin for two admissions

I want to listen to Verman — I *want* to — I WANT
to ——"

Wailing, she was borne away — of her sex not the
first to be fascinated by obscurity, nor the last to
champion its eloquence.

Verman was almost unendurable after this, but,
like many, many other managers, Schofield and
Williams restrained their choler, and even laughed
fulsomely when their principal attraction essayed
the rôle of a comedian in private, and capered and
squawked in sheer, fatuous vanity.

The first performance of the afternoon rivalled the
successes of the morning, and although Miss Rennsdale was detained at home, thus drying up the single
source of cash income developed before lunch, Maurice Levy appeared, escorting Marjorie Jones, and
paid coin for two admissions, dropping the money
into Sam's hand with a careless — nay, a contempt-
uous — gesture.   At sight of Marjorie, Penrod Schofield flushed under his new moustache (repainted
since noon) and lectured as he had never lectured
before.   A new grace invested his every gesture;
a new sonorousness rang in his voice; a simple and
manly pomposity marked his very walk as he
passed from curio to curio.   And when he fear-

lessly handled the box of rats and hammered upon
it with cool *insouciance*, he beheld — for the first
time in his life — a purl of admiration eddying in
Marjorie's lovely eye, a certain softening of that
eye. And then Verman spake — and Penrod was
forgotten. Marjorie's eye rested upon him no
more.

A heavily equipped chauffeur ascended the stairway, bearing the message that Mrs. Levy awaited
her son and his lady. Thereupon, having devoured the last sound permitted (by the managers)
to issue from Verman, Mr. Levy and Miss Jones
departed to a real matinée at a real theatre, the
limpid eyes of Marjorie looking back softly over her
shoulder — but only at the tattooed wild boy.
Nearly always it is woman who puts the irony into
life.

After this, perhaps because of sated curiosity,
perhaps on account of a pin famine, the attendance
began to languish. Only four responded to the next
call of the band; the four dwindled to three; finally
the entertainment was given for one *blasé* auditor,
and Schofield and Williams looked depressed. Then
followed an interval when the band played in vain.

About three o'clock Schofield and Williams were

gloomily discussing various unpromising devices for startling the public into a renewal of interest, when another patron unexpectedly appeared and paid a cent for his admission. News of the Big Show and Museum of Curiosities had at last penetrated the far, cold spaces of interstellar niceness, for this new patron consisted of no less than Roderick Magsworth Bitts, Junior, escaped in a white "sailor suit" from the Manor during a period of severe maternal and tutorial preoccupation.

He seated himself without parley, and the pufformance was offered for his entertainment with admirable conscientiousness. True to the Lady Clara caste and training, Roderick's pale, fat face expressed nothing except an impervious superiority and, as he sat, cold and unimpressed upon the front bench, like a large, white lump, it must be said that he made a discouraging audience "to play to." He was not, however, unresponsive — far from it. He offered comment very chilling to the warm grandiloquence of the orator.

"That's my uncle Ethelbert's dachshund," he remarked, at the beginning of the lecture. "You better take him back if you don't want to get arrested." And when Penrod, rather uneasily ignoring the interruption, proceeded to the exploitation of the genuine, full-blooded Indian dog, Duke, "Why don't you try to give that old dog away?" asked Roderick. "You couldn't sell him."

"My papa would buy me a lots better 'coon than that," was the information volunteered a little later, "only I wouldn't want the nasty old thing."

Herman of the missing finger obtained no greater indulgence. "Pooh!" said Roderick. "We have two fox-terriers in our stables that took prizes at the kennel show, and their tails were *bit* off. There's a man that always bites fox-terriers' tails off."

"Oh, my gosh, what a lie!" exclaimed Sam Williams ignorantly. "Go on with the show whether he likes it or not, Penrod. He's paid his money."

Verman, confident in his own singular powers, chuckled openly at the failure of the other attractions to charm the frosty visitor, and, when his turn came, poured forth a torrent of conversation which was straightway dammed.

"Rotten," said Mr. Bitts languidly. "Anybody could talk like that. *I* could do it if I wanted to."

Verman paused suddenly.

"*Yes*, you could?" exclaimed Penrod, stung. "Let's hear you do it, then."

"Yessir!" the other partner shouted. "Let's just hear you *do* it!"

"I said I could if I wanted to," responded Roderick, "I didn't say I *would*."

"Yay! Knows he can't!" sneered Sam.

"I can, too, if I try."

"Well, let's hear you try!"

So challenged, the visitor did try, but, in the absence of an impartial jury, his effort was considered so pronounced a failure that he was howled down, derided, and mocked with great clamours.

"Anyway," said Roderick, when things had quieted down, "if I couldn't get up a better show than this I'd sell out and leave town."

Not having enough presence of mind to inquire what he would sell out, his adversaries replied with mere formless yells of scorn.

"I could get up a better show than this with my left hand," Roderick asserted.

"Well, what would you have in your ole show?" asked Penrod, condescending to language.

"That's all right, what I'd *have*. I'd have enough!"

"You couldn't get Herman and Verman in *your* ole show."

"No, and I wouldn't want 'em, either!"

"Well, what *would* you have?" insisted Penrod derisively. "You'd have to have *sumpthing* — you couldn't be a show yourself!"

"How do *you* know?" This was but meandering while waiting for ideas, and evoked another yell.

"You think you could be a show all by yourself?" demanded Penrod.

"How do *you* know I couldn't?"

Two white boys and two black boys shrieked their scorn of the boaster.

"I could, too!" Roderick raised his voice to a sudden howl, obtaining a hearing.

"Well, why don't you tell us how?"

"Well, *I* know *how*, all right," said Roderick. "If anybody asks you, you can just tell him I know *how*, all right."

"Why, you can't *do* anything," Sam began argumentatively. "You talk about being a show all by yourself; what could you try to do? Show us sumpthing you can do."

"I didn't say I was going to *do* anything," returned the badgered one, still evading.

"Well, then, how'd you *be* a show?" Penrod demanded. "*We* got a show here, even if Herman didn't point or Verman didn't talk. Their father stabbed a man with a pitchfork, I guess, didn't he?"

"How do *I* know?"

"Well, I guess he's in jail, ain't he?"

"Well, what if their father is in jail? I didn't say he wasn't, did I?"

"Well, *your* father ain't in jail, is he?"

"Well, I never said he was, did I?"

"Well, then," continued Penrod, "how could you be a ——" He stopped abruptly, staring at Roderick, the birth of an idea plainly visible in his altered expression. He had suddenly remembered his intention to ask Roderick Magsworth Bitts, Junior, about Rena Magsworth, and this recollection collided in his mind with the irritation produced by Roderick's claiming some mysterious attainment which would warrant his setting up as a show in his single person. Penrod's whole manner changed instantly.

"Roddy," he asked, almost overwhelmed by a prescience of something vast and magnificent, "Roddy, are you any relation of Rena Magsworth?"

Roderick had never heard of Rena Magsworth, although a concentration of the sentence yesterday pronounced upon her had burned, black and horrific, upon the face of every newspaper in the country.

He was not allowed to read the journals of the day, and his family's indignation over the sacrilegious coincidence of the name had not been expressed in his presence. But he saw that it was an awesome name to Penrod Schofield and Samuel Williams. Even Herman and Verman, though lacking many educational advantages on account of a long residence in the country, were informed on the subject of Rena Magsworth through hearsay, and they joined in the portentous silence.

"Roddy," repeated Penrod, "honest, is Rena Magsworth some relation of yours?"

There is no obsession more dangerous to its victims than a conviction — especially an inherited one — of superiority: this world is so full of Missourians. And from his earliest years Roderick Magsworth Bitts, Junior, had been trained to believe in the importance of the Magsworth family. At every meal he absorbed a sense of Magsworth greatness, and yet, in his infrequent meetings with persons of his own age and sex, he was treated as negligible. Now, dimly, he perceived that there was a Magsworth claim of some sort which was impressive, even to boys. Magsworth blood was the essential of all true distinction in the world, he knew. Consequently, having been driven into a *cul-de-sac*, as a result of flagrant and unfounded boasting, he was ready to take advantage of what appeared to be a triumphal way out.

"Roddy," said Penrod again, with solemnity, "is Rena Magsworth some relation of yours?"

"*Is* she, Roddy?" asked Sam, almost hoarsely.

"She's my aunt!" shouted Roddy.

Silence followed. Sam and Penrod, spellbound, gazed upon Roderick Magsworth Bitts, Junior. So did Herman and Verman. Roddy's staggering lie had changed the face of things utterly. No one questioned it; no one realized that it was much too good to be true.

"Roddy," said Penrod, in a voice tremulous with hope, "Roddy, will you join our show?"

Roddy joined.

Even he could see that the offer implied his being starred as the paramount attraction of a new order of things. It was obvious that he had swelled out suddenly, in the estimation of the other boys, to that importance which he had been taught to believe his native gift and natural right. The sensation was pleasant. He had often been treated with effusion by grown-up callers and by acquaintances of his

mother and sisters; he had heard ladies speak of
him as "charming" and "that delightful child,"
and little girls had sometimes shown him deference,
but until this moment no boy had ever allowed him,
for one moment, to presume even to equality. Now,
in a trice, he was not only admitted to comradeship,
but patently valued as something rare and sacred,
to be acclaimed and pedestalled. In fact, the very
first thing that Schofield and Williams did was to
find a box for him to stand upon.

The misgivings roused in Roderick's bosom by
the subsequent activities of the firm were not bother-
some enough to make him forego his prominence
as Exhibit A. He was not a "quick-minded" boy,
and it was long (and much happened) before he
thoroughly comprehended the causes of his new
celebrity. He had a shadowy feeling that if the
affair came to be heard of at home it might not be
liked, but, intoxicated by the glamour and bustle
which surround a public character, he made no
protest. On the contrary, he entered whole-heartedly into the preparations for the new show. Assuming, with Sam's assistance, a blue moustache
and "sideburns," he helped in the painting of a new
poster, which, supplanting the old one on the wall

of the stable facing the cross-street, screamed bloody murder at the passers in that rather populous thoroughfare.

SCHoFiELD & WiLLiAMS
NEW BIG SHoW
RoDERiCK MAGSWoRTH BiTTS JR

ONLY LiViNG NEPHEW

oF
RENA MAGSWORTH
THE FAMOS

MUDERESS GoiNG To BE HUNG
NEXT JULY KiLED EiGHT PEOPLE
PUT ARSiNECK iN THiER MiLK ALSO
SHERMAN HERMAN AND VERMAN
THE MiCHiGAN RATS DOG PART
ALLiGATOR DUKE THE GENUiNE
InDiAN DoG ADMiSSioN 1 CENT oR
20 PiNS SAME AS BEFORE Do NoT
MiSS THiS CHANSE TO SEE RoD-
ERiCK
ONLY LiViNG NEPHEW oF RENA
MAGSWORTH THE GREAT FAMOS
MUDERESS
GoiNG To BE
HUNG

CHAPTER XVII

MEGAPHONES were constructed out of heavy wrapping-paper, and Penrod, Sam, and Herman set out in different directions, delivering vocally the inflammatory proclamation of the poster to a large section of the residential quarter, and leaving Roderick Magsworth Bitts, Junior, with Verman in the loft, shielded from all deadhead eyes. Upon the return of the heralds, the Schofield and Williams Military Band played deafeningly, and an awakened public once more thronged to fill the coffers of the firm.

[167

Prosperity smiled again. The very first audience after the acquisition of Roderick was larger than the largest of the morning. Master Bitts — the only exhibit placed upon a box — was a supercurio. All eyes fastened upon him and remained, hungrily feasting, throughout Penrod's luminous oration.

But the glory of one light must ever be the dimming of another. We dwell in a vale of seesaws — and cobwebs spin fastest upon laurel. Verman, the tattooed wild boy, speaking only in his native foreign languages, Verman the gay, Verman the caperer, capered no more; he chuckled no more, he beckoned no more, nor tapped his chest, nor wreathed his idolatrous face in smiles. Gone, all gone, were his little artifices for attracting the general attention to himself; gone was every engaging mannerism which had endeared him to the mercurial public. He squatted against the wall and glowered at the new sensation. It was the old story — the old, old story of too much temperament: Verman was suffering from artistic jealousy.

The second audience contained a cash-paying adult, a spectacled young man whose poignant attention was very flattering. He remained after the lecture, and put a few questions to Roddy, which were answered rather confusedly upon promptings from Penrod. The young man went away without having stated the object of his interrogations, but it became quite plain, later in the day. This same object caused the spectacled young man to make several brief but stimulating calls directly after leaving the Schofield and Williams Big Show, and the consequences thereof loitered not by the wayside.

The Big Show was at high tide. Not only was the auditorium filled and throbbing; there was an indubitable line — by no means wholly juvenile — waiting for admission to the next pufformance. A group stood in the street examining the poster earnestly as it glowed in the long, slanting rays of the westward sun, and people in automobiles and other vehicles had halted wheel in the street to read the message so piquantly given to the world. These were the conditions when a crested victoria arrived at a gallop, and a large, chastely magnificent and highly flushed woman descended, and progressed across the yard with an air of violence.

At sight of her, the adults of the waiting line hastily disappeared, and most of the pausing vehicles moved instantly on their way. She was followed by a stricken man in livery.

The stairs to the auditorium were narrow and steep; Mrs. Roderick Magsworth Bitts was of a stout favour; and the voice of Penrod was audible during the ascent.

"*Re-mem-bur*, gentilmun and lay-deeze, each and all are now gazing upon Roderick Magsworth Bitts, Junior, the only living nephew of the great Rena Magsworth. She stuck ars'nic in the milk of eight separate and distinck people to put in their coffee and each and all of 'em died. The great ars'nic murderess, Rena Magsworth, gentilmun and lay-deeze, and Roddy's her only living nephew. She's a relation of all the Bitts family, but he's her one and only living nephew. Re-*mem*-bur! Next July she's goin' to be hung, and, each and all, you now see before you ———"

Penrod paused abruptly, seeing something before himself — the august and awful presence which filled the entryway. And his words (it should be related) froze upon his lips.

Before *her*self, Mrs. Roderick Magsworth Bitts saw her son — her scion — wearing a moustache and sideburns of blue, and perched upon a box flanked by Sherman and Verman, the Michigan rats, the Indian dog Duke, Herman, and the dog part alligator.

Roddy, also, saw something before himself. It needed no prophet to read the countenance of the dread apparition in the entryway. His mouth opened — remained open — then filled to capacity with a calamitous sound of grief not unmingled with apprehension.

Penrod's reason staggered under the crisis. For a horrible moment he saw Mrs. Roderick Magsworth Bitts approaching like some fatal mountain in avalanche. She seemed to grow larger and redder; lightnings played about her head; he had a vague consciousness of the audience spraying out in flight, of the squealings, tramplings and dispersals of a stricken field. The mountain was close upon him——

He stood by the open mouth of the hay-chute which went through the floor to the manger below. Penrod also went through the floor. He propelled himself into the chute and shot down, but not quite to the manger, for Mr. Samuel Williams had thoughtfully stepped into the chute a moment in advance of his partner. Penrod lit upon Sam.

Catastrophic noises resounded in the loft; volcanoes seemed to romp upon the stairway.

There ensued a period when only a shrill keen-

ing marked the passing of Roderick as he was borne
to the tumbril.   Then all was silence.

. . . Sunset, striking through a western window, rouged the walls of the Schofields' library,
where gathered a joint family council and court mar-
tial of four — Mrs. Schofield, Mr. Schofield, and
Mr. and Mrs. Williams, parents of Samuel of that
ilk.   Mr. Williams read aloud a conspicuous passage from the last edition of the evening paper:

"Prominent people here believed close relations
of woman sentenced to hang.   Angry denial by
Mrs. R. Magsworth Bitts.   Relationship admitted
by younger member of family.   His statement confirmed by boy-friends ——"

"Don't!" said Mrs. Williams, addressing her
husband vehemently.   "We've all read it a dozen
times.   We've got plenty of trouble on our hands
without hearing *that* again!"

Singularly enough, Mrs. Williams did not look
troubled; she looked as if she were trying to look
troubled.   Mrs. Schofield wore a similar expression.
So did Mr. Schofield.   So did Mr. Williams.

"What did she say when she called *you* up?" Mrs.
Schofield inquired breathlessly of Mrs. Williams.

"She could hardly speak at first, and then when she did talk, she talked so fast I couldn't understand most of it, and ——"

"It was just the same when she tried to talk to me," said Mrs. Schofield, nodding.

"I never did hear any one in such a state before," continued Mrs. Williams. "So furious ——"

"Quite justly, of course," said Mrs. Schofield.

"Of course. And she said Penrod and Sam had enticed Roderick away from home — usually he's not allowed to go outside the yard except with his tutor or a servant — and had told him to say that horrible creature was his aunt ——"

"How in the world do you suppose Sam and Penrod ever thought of such a thing as *that!*" exclaimed Mrs. Schofield. "It must have been made up just for their 'show.' Della says there were just *streams* going in and out all day. Of course it wouldn't have happened, but this was the day Margaret and I spend every month in the country with Aunt Sarah, and I didn't *dream* ——"

"She said one thing I thought rather tactless," interrupted Mrs. Williams. "Of course we must allow for her being dreadfully excited and wrought up, but I do think it wasn't quite delicate in her,

and she's usually the very soul of delicacy. She
said that Roderick had *never* been allowed to asso-
ciate with — with common boys ——"

"Meaning Sam and Penrod," said Mrs. Schofield.
"Yes, she said that to me, too."

"She said that the most awful thing about it,"
Mrs. Williams went on, "was that, though she's
going to prosecute the newspapers, many people
would always believe the story, and ——"

"Yes, I imagine they will," said Mrs. Schofield
musingly. "Of course you and I and everybody
who really knows the Bitts and Magsworth families
understand the perfect absurdity of it; but I suppose
there are ever so many who'll believe it, no matter
what the Bittses and Magsworths say."

"Hundreds and hundreds!" said Mrs. Williams.
"I'm afraid it will a be great come-down for them."

"I'm afraid so," said Mrs. Schofield gently. "A
very great one — yes, a very, very great one."

"Well," observed Mrs. Williams, after a thoughtful pause, "there's only one thing to be done, and I
suppose it had better be done right away."

She glanced toward the two gentlemen.

"Certainly," Mr. Schofield agreed. "But where
are they?"

"Have you looked in the stable?" asked his wife.

"I searched it. They've probably started for the Far West."

"Did you look in the sawdust-box?"

"No, I didn't."

"Then that's where they are."

Thus, in the early twilight, the now historic stable was approached by two fathers charged to do the only thing to be done. They entered the storeroom.

"Penrod!" said Mr. Schofield.

"Sam!" said Mr. Williams.

Nothing disturbed the twilight hush.

But by means of a ladder, brought from the carriage-house, Mr. Schofield mounted to the top of the sawdust-box. He looked within, and discerned the dim outlines of three quiet figures, the third being that of a small dog.

The two boys rose, upon command, descended the ladder after Mr. Schofield, bringing Duke with them, and stood before the authors of their being, who bent upon them sinister and threatening brows. With hanging heads and despondent countenances, each still ornamented with a moustache and an imperial, Penrod and Sam awaited sentence.

This is a boy's lot: anything he does, anything

whatever, may afterward turn out to have been a crime — he never knows.

And punishment and clemency are alike inexplicable.

Mr. Williams took his son by the ear.

"You march home!" he commanded.

Sam marched, not looking back, and his father followed the small figure implacably.

"You goin' to whip me?" quavered Penrod, alone with Justice.

"Wash your face at that hydrant," said his father sternly.

About fifteen minutes later, Penrod, hurriedly entering the corner drug store, two blocks distant, was astonished to perceive a familiar form at the soda counter.

"Yay, Penrod," said Sam Williams. "Want some sody? Come on. He didn't lick me. He didn't do anything to me at all. He gave me a quarter."

"So'd mine," said Penrod.

CHAPTER XVIII

MUSIC

BOYHOOD is the longest time in life — for a boy. The last term of the school-year is made of decades, not of weeks, and living through them is like waiting for the millennium. But they do pass, somehow, and at last there came a day when Penrod was one of a group that capered out from the gravelled yard of "Ward School, Nomber Seventh," carolling a leave-taking of the institution, of their instructress, and not even forgetting Mr. Capps, the janitor.

> "Good-bye, teacher!   Good-bye, school!
> Good-bye, Cappsie, dern ole fool!"

177

Penrod sang the loudest. For every boy, there is an age when he "finds his voice." Penrod's had not "changed," but he had found it. Inevitably that thing had come upon his family and the neighbours; and his father, a somewhat dyspeptic man, quoted frequently the expressive words of the "Lady of Shalott," but there were others whose sufferings were as poignant.

Vacation-time warmed the young of the world to pleasant languor; and a morning came that was like a brightly coloured picture in a child's fairy story. Miss Margaret Schofield, reclining in a hammock upon the front porch, was beautiful in the eyes of a newly made senior, well favoured and in fair raiment, beside her. A guitar rested lightly upon his knee, and he was trying to play — a matter of some difficulty, as the floor of the porch also seemed inclined to be musical. From directly under his feet came a voice of song, shrill, loud, incredibly piercing and incredibly flat, dwelling upon each syllable with incomprehensible reluctance to leave it.

> "I have lands and earthly pow-wur.
> I'd give all for a now-wur,
> Whi-ilst setting at *my-y-y* dear old mother's knee-ee,
> So-o-o rem-mem-bur whilst you're young ——"

Miss Schofield stamped heartily upon the musical floor.

"It's Penrod," she explained. "The lattice at the end of the porch is loose, and he crawls under and comes out all bugs. He's been having a dreadful singing fit lately — running away to picture shows and vaudeville, I suppose."

Mr. Robert Williams looked upon her yearningly. He touched a thrilling chord on his guitar and leaned nearer. "But you said you *have* missed me," he began. "I ——"

The voice of Penrod drowned all other sounds.

> "So-o-o rem-mem-bur, whi-i-ilst you're young,
>   That the da-a-ys to you will come,
>   When you're o-o-old and only in the way.
>   Do not scoff at them *bee*-cause ——"

"*Penrod!*" Miss Schofield stamped again.

"You *did* say you'd missed me," said Mr. Robert Williams, seizing hurriedly upon the silence. "Didn't you say ——"

A livelier tune rose upward.

> "Oh, you talk about your fascinating beauties,
>   Of your dem-*o*-zells, your belles,
>   But the littil dame I met, while in the city,

She's par excellaws the queen of all the swells.
She's sweeter far ——"

Margaret rose and jumped up and down repeatedly in a well-calculated area, whereupon the voice of Penrod cried chokedly, "*Quit* that!" and there were subterranean coughings and sneezings.

"You want to choke a person to death?" he inquired severely, appearing at the end of the porch, a cobweb upon his brow. And, continuing, he put into practice a newly acquired phrase, "You better learn to be more considerick of other people's comfort."

Slowly and grievedly he withdrew, passed to the sunny side of the house, reclined in the warm grass beside his wistful Duke, and presently sang again.

"She's sweeter far than the flower I named her after,
    And the memery of her smile it haunts me YET!
When in after years the moon is soffly beamun'
    And at eve I smell the smell of mignonette
I will re-CALL that —— "

"Pen-*rod!*"

Mr. Schofield appeared at an open window upstairs, a book in his hand.

"Stop it!" he commanded. "Can't I stay home

with a headache *one* morning from the office without
having to listen to — I never *did* hear such squawk-
ing!" He retired from the window, having too im-
pulsively called upon his Maker. Penrod, shocked
and injured, entered the house, but presently his
voice was again audible as far as the front porch.
He was holding converse with his mother, somewhere
in the interior.

"Well, what of it? Sam Williams told me his
mother said if Bob ever did think of getting married
to Margaret, his mother said she'd like to know
what in the name o' goodness they expect to ——"

Bang! Margaret thought it better to close the
front door.

The next minute Penrod opened it. "I suppose
you want the whole family to get a sunstroke," he
said reprovingly. "Keepin' every breath of air
out o' the house on a day like this!"

And he sat down implacably in the doorway.

The serious poetry of all languages has omitted
the little brother; and yet he is one of the great trials
of love — the immemorial burden of courtship.
Tragedy should have found place for him, but he
has been left to the haphazard vignettist of Grub
Street. He is the grave and real menace of lovers:

his head is sacred and terrible, his power illimitable.
There is one way — only one — to deal with him;
but Robert Williams, having a brother of Penrod's
age, understood that way.

Robert had one dollar in the world. He gave it
to Penrod immediately.

Enslaved forever, the new Rockefeller rose and
went forth upon the highway, an overflowing heart
bursting the floodgates of song.

"In her eyes the light of love was soffly gleamun',
      So sweetlay,
      So neatlay.
  On the banks the moon's soff light was brightly
        streamun',
      Words of love I then spoke *to* her,
      She was purest of the *pew*-er:
  'Littil sweetheart, do not sigh,
  Do not weep and do not cry.
  I will build a littil cottige just for yew-*ew*-EW and I.' "

In fairness, it must be called to mind that boys
older than Penrod have these wellings of pent mel-
ody: a wife can never tell when she is to undergo a
musical morning, and even the golden wedding
brings her no security' a man of ninety is liable to
bust-loose in song, any time.

Invalids murmured pitifully as Penrod came within hearing; and people trying to think cursed the day that they were born, when he went shrilling by. His hands in his pockets, his shining face uplifted to the sky of June, he passed down the street, singing his way into the heart's deepest hatred of all who heard him.

> "One evuning I was sturow-ling
>   Midst the city of the *Dead*,
> I viewed where all a-round me
>   Their *peace*-full graves was SPREAD.
> But that which touched me mostlay ——"

He had reached his journey's end, a junk-dealer's shop wherein lay the long-desired treasure of his soul — an accordion which might have possessed a high quality of interest for an antiquarian, being unquestionably a ruin, beautiful in decay, and quite beyond the sacrilegious reach of the restorer. But it was still able to disgorge sounds — loud, strange, compelling sounds, which could be heard for a remarkable distance in all directions; and it had one rich calf-like tone that had gone to Penrod's heart. He obtained the instrument for twenty-two cents, a price long since agreed upon with the junk-dealer, who falsely claimed a loss of profit, Shylock that he was! He had found the wreck in an alley.

With this purchase suspended from his shoulder by a faded green cord, Penrod set out in a somewhat homeward direction, but not by the route he had just travelled, though his motive for the change was not humanitarian. It was his desire to display himself thus troubadouring to the gaze of Marjorie Jones. Heralding his advance by continuous experiments in the music of the future, he pranced upon his blithesome way, the faithful Duke at his heels. (It was easier for Duke than it would have been for a younger dog, because, with advancing age, he had begun to grow a little deaf.)

Turning the corner nearest to the glamoured mansion of the Joneses, the boy jongleur came suddenly face to face with Marjorie, and, in the delicious surprise of the encounter, ceased to play, his hands, in agitation, falling from the instrument.

Bareheaded, the sunshine glorious upon her amber curls, Marjorie was strolling hand-in-hand with her baby brother, Mitchell, four years old. She wore pink that day — unforgettable pink, with a broad, black patent-leather belt, shimmering reflections dancing upon its surface. How beautiful she was!

How sacred the sweet little baby brother, whose privilege it was to cling to that small hand, delicately powdered with freckles.

"Hello, Marjorie," said Penrod, affecting carelessness.

"Hello!" said Marjorie, with unexpected cordiality. She bent over her baby brother with motherly affectations. "Say 'howdy' to the gentymuns, Mitchy-Mitch," she urged sweetly, turning him to face Penrod.

"*Won't!*" said Mitchy-Mitch, and, to emphasize his refusal, kicked the gentymuns upon the shin.

Penrod's feelings underwent instant change, and in the sole occupation of disliking Mitchy-Mitch, he wasted precious seconds which might have been better employed in philosophic consideration of the startling example, just afforded, of how a given law operates throughout the universe in precisely the same manner perpetually. Mr. Robert Williams would have understood this, easily.

"Oh, oh!" Marjorie cried, and put Mitchy-Mitch behind her with too much sweetness. "Maurice Levy's gone to Atlantic City with his mamma," she remarked conversationally, as if the kicking incident were quite closed.

"That's nothin'," returned Penrod, keeping his eye uneasily upon Mitchy-Mitch. "I know plenty people been better places than that — Chicago and everywhere."

There was unconscious ingratitude in his low rating of Atlantic City, for it was largely to the attractions of that resort he owed Miss Jones' present attitude of friendliness. Of course, too, she was curious about the accordion. It would be dastardly to hint that she had noticed a paper bag which bulged the pocket of Penrod's coat, and yet this bag was undeniably conspicuous — "and children are very like grown people, sometimes!"

Penrod brought forth the bag, purchased on the way at a drug store, and till this moment *unopened*, which expresses in a word the depth of his sentiment for Marjorie. It contained an abundant fifteen-cents' worth of lemon drops, jaw-breakers, licorice sticks, cinnamon drops, and shopworn chocolate creams.

"Take all you want," he said, with off-hand generosity.

"Why, Penrod Schofield," exclaimed the wholly thawed damsel, "you nice boy!"

"Oh, that's nothin'," he returned airily. "I got a good deal of money, nowadays."

"Where from?"

"Oh — just around." With a cautious gesture he offered a jaw-breaker to Mitchy-Mitch, who snatched it indignantly and set about its absorption without delay.

"Can you play on that?" asked Marjorie, with some difficulty, her cheeks being rather too hilly for conversation.

"Want to hear me?"

She nodded, her eyes sweet with anticipation.

This was what he had come for. He threw back his head, lifted his eyes dreamily, as he had seen real musicians lift theirs, and distended the accordion preparing to produce the wonderful calf-like noise which was the instrument's great charm. But the distention evoked a long wail which was at once drowned in another one.

"Ow! Owowaoh! Wowohah! Waow*wow!*" shrieked Mitchy-Mitch and the accordion together.

Mitchy-Mitch, to emphasize his disapproval of the accordion, opening his mouth still wider, lost therefrom the jaw-breaker, which rolled in the dust. Weeping, he stooped to retrieve it, and Marjorie, to prevent him, hastily set her foot upon it. Penrod offered another jaw-breaker; but Mitchy-Mitch struck it from his hand, desiring the former, which had convinced him of its sweetness.

Marjorie moved inadvertently; whereupon Mitchy-Mitch pounced upon the remains of his jaw-breaker and restored them, with accretions, to his mouth. His sister, uttering a cry of horror, sprang to the rescue, assisted by Penrod, whom she prevailed upon to hold Mitchy-Mitch's mouth open while she excavated. This operation being completed, and Penrod's right thumb severely bitten, Mitchy-Mitch closed his eyes tightly, stamped, squealed, bellowed, wrung his hands, and then, unexpectedly, kicked Penrod again.

Penrod put a hand in his pocket and drew forth a copper two-cent piece, large, round, and fairly bright.

He gave it to Mitchy-Mitch.

Mitchy-Mitch immediately stopped crying and gazed upon his benefactor with the eyes of a dog.

This world!

Thereafter did Penrod — with complete approval from Mitchy-Mitch — play the accordion for his lady to his heart's content, and hers. Never had he so won upon her; never had she let him feel so close to her before. They strolled up and down upon the sidewalk, eating, one thought between them,

Never had he so won upon her; never had she let him feel so close to her before

and soon she had learned to play the accordion almost as well as he.   So passed a happy hour, which the Good King René of Anjou would have envied them, while Mitchy-Mitch made friends with Duke, romped about his sister and her swain, and clung to the hand of the latter, at intervals, with fondest affection and trust.

The noon whistles failed to disturb this little Arcady; only the sound of Mrs. Jones' voice — for the third time summoning Marjorie and Mitchy-Mitch to lunch — sent Penrod on his way.

"I could come back this afternoon, I guess," he said, in parting.

"I'm not goin' to be here.   I'm goin' to Baby Rennsdale's party."

Penrod looked blank, as she intended he should. Having thus satisfied herself, she added:

"There aren't goin' to be any boys there."

He was instantly radiant again.

"Marjorie ——"

"Hum?"

"Do you wish I was goin' to be there?"

She looked shy, and turned away her head.

"*Marjorie Jones!*"   (This was a voice from home.)
"*How many more times shall I have to call you?*"

Marjorie moved away, her face still hidden from Penrod.

"Do you?" he urged.

At the gate, she turned quickly toward him, and said over her shoulder, all in a breath: "Yes! Come again to-morrow morning and I'll be on the corner. Bring your 'cordion!"

And she ran into the house, Mitchy-Mitch waving a loving hand to the boy on the sidewalk until the front door closed.

CHAPTER XIX

THE INNER BOY

PENROD went home in splendour, pretend. ing that he and Duke were a long procession; and he made enough noise to render the auricular part of the illusion perfect. His own family were already at the lunch-table when he arrived, and the parade halted only at the door of the dining-room.

"Oh *Something!*" shouted Mr. Schofield, clasping his bilious brow with both hands. "Stop that noise! Isn't it awful enough for you to *sing?* Sit *down!* Not with that thing on! Take that green rope off your shoulder! Now take that thing out of the dining-room and throw it in the ash-can! Where did you get it?"

"Where did I get what, papa?" asked Penrod meekly, depositing the accordion in the hall just outside the dining-room door.

"That da — that third-hand concertina."

"It's a 'cordion," said Penrod, taking his place at the table, and noticing that both Margaret and Mr. Robert Williams (who happened to be a guest) were growing red.

"I don't care what you call it," said Mr. Schofield irritably. "I want to know where you got it."

Penrod's eyes met Margaret's: hers had a strained expression. She very slightly shook her head. Penrod sent Mr. Williams a grateful look, and might have been startled if he could have seen himself in a mirror at that moment; for he regarded Mitchy-Mitch with concealed but vigorous aversion, and the resemblance would have horrified him.

"A man gave it to me," he answered gently, and was rewarded by the visibly regained ease of his patron's manner, while Margaret leaned back in her chair and looked at her brother with real devotion.

"I should think he'd have been glad to," said Mr. Schofield. "Who was he?"

"Sir?" In spite of the candy which he had consumed in company with Marjorie and Mitchy-Mitch, Penrod had begun to eat lobster croquettes earnestly.

"Who *was* he?"

"Who do you mean, papa?"

"The man that gave you that ghastly Thing!"

"Yessir. A man gave it to me."

"I say, Who *was* he?" shouted Mr. Schofield.

"Well, I was just walking along, and the man came up to me — it was right down in front of Colgates', where most of the paint's rubbed off the fence ——"

"Penrod!" The father used his most dangerous tone.

"Sir?"

"Who was the man that gave you the concertina?"

"I don't know. I was walking along and ——."

"You never saw him before?"

"No, sir. I was just walk ——"

"That will do," said Mr. Schofield, rising. "I suppose every family has its secret enemies and this was one of ours. I must ask to be excused!"

With that, he went out crossly, stopping in the hall a moment before passing beyond hearing. And, after lunch, Penrod sought in vain for his accordion; he even searched the library where his father sat reading, though, upon inquiry, Penrod explained that he was looking for a misplaced school-book. He thought he ought to study a little every day, he said, even during vacation-time. Much pleased, Mr. Schofield rose and joined the search, finding the missing work on mathematics with singular ease — which cost him precisely the price of the book the following September.

Penrod departed to study in the backyard. There, after a cautious survey of the neighbourhood, he managed to dislodge the iron cover of the cistern, and dropped the arithmetic within. A fine splash rewarded his listening ear. Thus assured that when he looked for that book again no one would find it for him, he replaced the cover, and betook himself pensively to the highway, discouraging Duke from following by repeated volleys of stones, some imaginary and others all too real.

Distant strains of brazen horns and the throbbing of drums were borne to him upon the kind breeze, reminding him that the world was made for joy, and that the Barzee and Potter Dog and Pony Show was exhibiting in a banlieue not far away. So, thither he bent his steps — the plentiful funds in his pocket burning hot holes all the way. He had paid twenty-two cents for the accordion, and fifteen for candy; he had bought the mercenary heart of Mitchy-Mitch for two: it certainly follows that there remained to him of his dollar, sixty-one cents — a fair fortune, and most unusual.

Arrived upon the populous and festive scene of the Dog and Pony Show, he first turned his attention to the brightly decorated booths which surrounded the tent. The cries of the peanut vendors, of the popcorn men, of the toy-balloon sellers, the stirring music of the band, playing before the performance to attract a crowd, the shouting of excited children and the barking of the dogs within the tent, all sounded exhilaratingly in Penrod's ears and set his blood a-tingle. Nevertheless, he did not squander his money or fling it to the winds in one grand splurge. Instead, he began cautiously with the purchase of an extraordinarily large pickle, which he obtained from an aged negress for his odd cent, too obvious a bargain to be missed. At an adjacent stand he bought a glass of raspberry lemonade (so alleged) and sipped it as he ate the pickle. He left nothing of either.

Next, he entered a small restaurant-tent and for a modest nickel was supplied with a fork and a box of sardines, previously opened, it is true, but more than half full. He consumed the sardines utterly, but left the tin box and the fork, after which he indulged in an inexpensive half-pint of lukewarm cider, at one of the open booths. Mug in hand, a gentle glow radiating toward his surface from various centres of activity deep inside him, he paused for breath — and the cool, sweet cadences of the watermelon man fell delectably upon his ear:

"Ice-cole *water*-melon; ice-cole water-*melon;* the biggest slice of *ice*-cole, ripe, red, *ice*-cole, rich an' rare; the biggest slice of ice-cole watermelon ever cut by the hand of man! *Buy* our *ice*-cole water-melon?"

Penrod, having drained the last drop of cider, complied with the watermelon man's luscious entreaty, and received a round slice of the fruit, magnificent in circumference and something over an inch in thickness. Leaving only the really dangerous part of the rind behind him, he wandered away from the vicinity of the watermelon man and supplied himself with a bag of peanuts, which, with the expenditure of a dime for admission, left a quarter still warm in his pocket. However, he managed to "break" the coin at a stand inside the tent, where a large, oblong paper box of popcorn was handed him, with twenty cents change. The box was too large to go into his pocket, but, having seated himself among some wistful Polack children, he placed it in his lap and devoured the contents at leisure during the performance. The popcorn was heavily larded with partially boiled molasses, and Penrod sandwiched mouthfuls of peanuts with gobs of this mass until the peanuts were all gone. After that, he ate with less avidity; a sense almost of satiety beginning to manifest itself to him, and it was not until the close of the performance that he disposed of the last morsel.

He descended a little heavily to the outflowing crowd in the arena, and bought a caterwauling toy balloon, but showed no great enthusiasm in manipulating it. Near the exit, as he came out, was a hot-waffle stand which he had overlooked, and a sense of duty obliged him to consume the three waffles, thickly powdered with sugar, which the waffle man cooked for him upon command.

They left a hottish taste in his mouth; they had not been quite up to his anticipation, indeed, and it was with a sense of relief that he turned to the "hokey-pokey" cart which stood close at hand, laden with square slabs of "Neapolitan ice-cream" wrapped in paper. He thought the ice-cream would be cooling, but somehow it fell short of the desired effect, and left a peculiar savour in his throat.

He walked away, too languid to blow his balloon, and passed a fresh-taffy booth with strange indifference. A bare-armed man was manipulating the taffy over a hook, pulling a great white mass to the desired stage of "candying," but Penrod did not pause to watch the operation; in fact, he averted his eyes (which were slightly glazed) in passing. He did not analyze his motives: simply, he was conscious that he preferred not to look at the mass of taffy.

For some reason, he put a considerable distance between himself and the taffy-stand, but before long halted in the presence of a red-faced man who flourished a long fork over a small cooking apparatus and shouted jovially: "Winnies! *Here's* your hot winnies! Hot winny-*wurst!* Food for the overworked brain, nourishing for the weak stummick, entertaining for the tired business man! *Here's* your hot winnies, three for a nickel, a half-a-dime, the twentieth-pot-of-a-dollah!'"

This, above all nectar and ambrosia, was the favourite dish of Penrod Schofield. Nothing inside him now craved it — on the contrary! But memory is the great hypnotist; his mind argued against his inwards that opportunity knocked at his door: "winny-wurst" was rigidly forbidden by the home authorities. Besides, there was a last nickel in his pocket; and nature protested against its survival. Also, the red-faced man had himself proclaimed his wares nourishing for the weak stummick.

Penrod placed the nickel in the red hand of the red-faced man.

He ate two of the three greasy, cigarlike shapes cordially pressed upon him in return. The first bite convinced him that he had made a mistake; these winnies seemed of a very inferior flavour, almost unpleasant, in fact. But he felt obliged to conceal his poor opinion of them, for fear of offending the red-faced man. He ate without haste or eagerness — so slowly, indeed, that he began to think the red-faced man might dislike him, as a deterrent of trade. Perhaps Penrod's mind was not working

The first bite convinced him that he had made a mistake

well, for he failed to remember that no law compelled him to remain under the eye of the red-faced man, but the virulent repulsion excited by his attempt to take a bite of the third sausage inspired him with at least an excuse for postponement.

"Mighty good," he murmured feebly, placing the sausage in the inside pocket of his jacket with a shaking hand. "Guess I'll save this one to eat at home, after — after dinner."

He moved sluggishly away, wishing he had not thought of dinner. A side-show, undiscovered until now, failed to arouse his interest, not even exciting a wish that he had known of its existence when he had money. For a time he stared without comprehension at a huge canvas poster depicting the chief attraction; the weather-worn colours conveying no meaning to his torpid eye. Then, little by little, the poster became more vivid to his consciousness. There was a greenish-tinted person in the tent, it seemed, who thrived upon a reptilian diet.

Suddenly, Penrod decided that it was time to go home.

CHAPTER XX

BROTHERS OF ANGELS

INDEED, doctor," said Mrs. Schofield, with
agitation and profound conviction, just after
eight o'clock that evening, "I shall *always*
believe in mustard plasters — mustard plasters and
hot-water bags. If it hadn't been for them I
don't believe he'd have *lived* till you got here —
I do *not!*"

"Margaret," called Mr. Schofield from the open
door of a bedroom, "Margaret, where did you put
that aromatic ammonia? Where's Margaret?"

But he had to find the aromatic spirits of ammonia himself, for Margaret was not in the house. She stood in the shadow beneath a maple tree near the street corner, a guitar-case in her hand; and she scanned with anxiety a briskly approaching figure. The arc light, swinging above, revealed this figure as that of him she awaited. He was passing toward the gate without seeing her, when she arrested him with a fateful whisper.

"*Bob!*"

Mr. Robert Williams swung about hastily. "Why, Margaret!"

"Here, take your guitar," she whispered hurriedly. "I was afraid if father happened to find it he'd break it all to pieces!"

"What for?" asked the startled Robert.

"Because I'm sure he knows it's yours."

"But what ——"

"Oh, Bob," she moaned, "I was waiting here to tell you. I was so afraid you'd try to come in ——"

"*Try!*" exclaimed the unfortunate young man, quite dumfounded. "*Try* to come ——"

"Yes, before I warned you. I've been waiting here to tell you, Bob, you mustn't come near the house — if I were you I'd stay away from even this neighbourhood — far away! For a while I don't think it would be actually *safe* for ——"

"Margaret, will you please ——"

"It's all on account of that dollar you gave Penrod this morning," she wailed. "First, he bought that horrible concertina that made papa so furious ——"

"But Penrod didn't tell that I ——"

"Oh, wait!" she cried lamentably. "Listen! He didn't tell at lunch, but he got home about dinner-time in the most — well! I've seen pale people before, but nothing like Penrod. Nobody could *imagine* it — not unless they'd seen him! And he looked so *strange*, and kept making such unnatural faces, and at first all he would say was that he'd eaten a little piece of apple and thought it must have had some microbes on it. But he got sicker and sicker, and we put him to bed — and then we all thought he was going to die — and, of *course*, no little piece of apple would have — well, and he kept getting worse — and then he said he'd had a dollar. He said he'd spent it for the concertina, and watermelon, and chocolate-creams, and licorice sticks, and lemon-drops, and peanuts, and jaw-breakers, and sardines, and raspberry lemonade, and pickles, and popcorn, and ice-cream, and cider, and sausage — there was sausage in his pocket, and mamma says his jacket is ruined — and cinnamon drops—and waffles—and he ate four or five lobster croquettes at lunch — and papa said, 'Who gave you that dollar?' Only he didn't say '*who*' — he said something horrible, Bob! And Penrod thought he was going to die, and he said *you* gave it to him, and oh! it was just pitiful to hear the poor child, Bob, because he thought he was dying, you see, and he blamed you for the whole thing. He said if you'd only let him alone and not given it to him, he'd have grown up to be a good man — and now he couldn't ! I never heard anything so heart-rending — he was so weak he could hardly whisper, but he kept trying to talk, telling us over and over it was all your fault."

In the darkness Mr. Williams' facial expression could not be seen, but his voice sounded hopeful.

"Is he — is he still in a great deal of pain?"

"They say the crisis is past," said Margaret, "but the doctor's still up there. He said it was the acutest case of indigestion he had ever treated in the whole course of his professional practice."

"Of course *I* didn't know what he'd do with the dollar," said Robert.

She did not reply.

He began plaintively, "Margaret, you don't ——"

"I've never seen papa and mamma so upset about anything," she said, rather primly.

"You mean they're upset about *me?*"

"We are *all* very much upset," returned Margaret, more starch in her ·tone as she remembered not only Penrod's sufferings but a duty she had vowed herself to perform.

"Margaret! *You* don't ——"

"Robert," she said firmly and, also, with a rhetorical complexity which breeds a suspicion of pre-rehearsal — "Robert, for the present I can only look at it in one way: when you gave that money to Penrod you put into the hands of an unthinking little child a weapon which might be, and, indeed was, the means of his undoing. Boys are not respon ——"

"But you saw me give him the dollar, and you didn't ——"

"Robert!" she checked him with increasing severity. "I am only a woman and not accustomed to thinking everything out on the spur of the moment; but I cannot change my mind. Not now, at least."

"And you think I'd better not come in to-night?"

"To-night!" she gasped. "Not for *weeks!* Papa would ——"

"But Margaret," he urged plaintively, "how can you blame me for ——"

"I have not used the word 'blame,' " she interrupted. "But I must insist that for your carelessness to — to wreak such havoc — cannot fail to — to lessen my confidence in your powers of judgment. I cannot change my convictions in this matter — not to-night — and I cannot remain here another instant. The poor child may need me. Robert, good-night."

With chill dignity she withdrew, entered the house, and returned to the sick-room, leaving the young man in outer darkness to brood upon his crime — and upon Penrod.

That sincere invalid became convalescent upon the third day; and a week elapsed, then, before he found an opportunity to leave the house unaccompanied — save by Duke. But at last he set forth and approached the Jones neighbourhood in high spirits, pleasantly conscious of his pallor, hollow cheeks, and other perquisites of illness provocative of interest.

One thought troubled him a little because it gave him a sense of inferiority to a rival. He believed, against his will, that Maurice Levy could have successfully eaten chocolate-creams, licorice sticks, lemon-drops, jaw-breakers, peanuts, waffles, lobster croquettes, sardines, cinnamon-drops, watermelon, pickles, popcorn, ice-cream and sausage with raspberry lemonade and cider. Penrod had admitted to himself that Maurice could do it and afterward attend to business, or pleasure, without the slightest discomfort; and this was probably no more than a fair estimate of one of the great constitutions of all time. As a digester, Maurice Levy would have disappointed a Borgia.

Fortunately, Maurice was still at Atlantic City — and now the convalescent's heart leaped. In the distance he saw Marjorie coming — in pink again, with a ravishing little parasol over her head. And alone! No Mitchy-Mitch was to mar this meeting.

Penrod increased the feebleness of his steps, now and then leaning upon the fence as if for support.

"How do you do, Marjorie?" he said, in his best sick-room voice, as she came near.

To his pained amazement, she proceeded on her way, her nose at a celebrated elevation — an icy nose.

She cut him dead.

He threw his invalid's airs to the winds, and hastened after her.

"Marjorie," he pleaded, "what's the matter? Are you mad? Honest, that day you said to come back next morning, and you'd be on the corner, I was sick. Honest, I was *awful* sick, Marjorie! I had to have the doctor ——"

"*Doctor!*" She whirled upon him, her lovely eyes blazing. "I guess *we've* had to have the doctor enough at *our* house, thanks to *you*, Mister Penrod Schofield. Papa says you haven't got *near* sense enough to come in out of the rain, after what you did to poor little Mitchy-Mitch ——"

"What?"

"Yes, and he's sick in bed *yet!*" Marjorie went on, with unabated fury. "And papa says if he ever catches you in this part of town ——"

"*What'd* I do to Mitchy-Mitch?" gasped Penrod.

"You know well enough what you did to Mitchy-Mitch!" she cried. "You gave him that great, big, nasty two-cent piece!"

"Well, what of it?"

"Mitchy-Mitch swallowed it!"

"What!"

"And papa says if he ever just lays eyes on you, once, in this neighbourhood ———"

But Penrod had started for home.

In his embittered heart there was increasing a critical disapproval of the Creator's methods. When He made pretty girls, thought Penrod, why couldn't He have left out their little brothers!

CHAPTER XXI

RUPE COLLINS

FOR several days after this, Penrod thought of growing up to be a monk, and engaged in good works so far as to carry some kittens (that otherwise would have been drowned) and a pair of Margaret's outworn dancing-slippers to a poor, ungrateful old man sojourning in a shed up the alley. And although Mr. Robert Williams, after a very short interval, began to leave his guitar on the front porch again, exactly as if he thought nothing had happened, Penrod, with his younger vision of a father's mood, remained coldly distant from the Jones neigh-

212

bourhood. With his own family his manner was gentle, proud and sad, but not for long enough to frighten them. The change came with mystifying abruptness at the end of the week.

It was Duke who brought it about.

Duke could chase a much bigger dog out of the Schofields' yard and far down the street. This might be thought to indicate unusual valour on the part of Duke and cowardice on that of the bigger dogs whom he undoubtedly put to rout. On the contrary, all such flights were founded in mere superstition, for dogs are even more superstitious than boys and coloured people; and the most firmly established of all dog superstitions is that any dog — be he the smallest and feeblest in the world — can whip any trespasser whatsoever.

A rat-terrier believes that on his home grounds he can whip an elephant. It follows, of course, that a big dog, away from his own home, will run from a little dog in the little dog's neighbourhood. Otherwise, the big dog must face a charge of inconsistency, and dogs are as consistent as they are superstitious. A dog believes in war, but he is convinced that there are times when it is moral to run; and the thoughtful physiognomist, seeing a big dog fleeing out of a

little dog's yard, must observe that the expression
of the big dog's face is more conscientious than
alarmed: it is the expression of a person performing a
duty to himself.

Penrod understood these matters perfectly; he knew
that the gaunt brown hound Duke chased up the alley
had fled only out of deference to a custom, yet Penrod
could not refrain from bragging of Duke to the
hound's owner, a fat-faced stranger of twelve or thirteen, who had wandered into the neighbourhood.

"You better keep that ole yellow dog o' yours
back," said Penrod ominously, as he climbed the
fence. "You better catch him and hold him till I
get mine inside the yard again. Duke's chewed
up some pretty bad bulldogs around here."

The fat-faced boy gave Penrod a fishy stare.
"You'd oughta learn him not to do that," he said,
"It'll make him sick."

"What will?"

The stranger laughed raspingly and gazed up the
alley, where the hound, having come to a halt, now
coolly sat down, and, with an expression of roguish
benevolence, patronizingly watched the tempered
fury of Duke, whose assaults and barkings were becoming perfunctory.

"What'll make Duke sick?" Penrod demanded.

"Eatin' dead bulldogs people leave around here."

This was not improvisation but formula, adapted from other occasions to the present encounter; nevertheless, it was new to Penrod, and he was so taken with it that resentment lost itself in admiration. Hastily committing the gem to memory for use upon a dog-owning friend, he inquired in a sociable tone:

"What's your dog's name?"

"Dan. You better call your ole pup, 'cause Dan eats *live* dogs."

Dan's actions poorly supported his master's assertion, for, upon Duke's ceasing to bark, Dan rose and showed the most courteous interest in making the little, old dog's acquaintance. Dan had a great deal of manner, and it became plain that Duke was impressed favourably in spite of former prejudice, so that presently the two trotted amicably back to their masters and sat down with the harmonious but indifferent air of having known each other intimately for years.

They were received without comment, though both boys looked at them reflectively for a time. It was Penrod who spoke first.

"What number you go to?" (In an "oral lesson in English," Penrod had been instructed to put this question in another form: "May I ask which of our public schools you attend?")

"Me? What number do I go to?" said the stranger, contemptuously. "I don't go to *no* number in vacation!"

"I mean when it ain't."

"Third," returned the fat-faced boy. "I got 'em *all* scared in *that* school."

"What of?" innocently asked Penrod, to whom "the Third" — in a distant part of town — was undiscovered country.

"What of? I guess you'd soon see what of, if you ever was in that school about one day. You'd be lucky if you got out alive!"

"Are the teachers mean?"

The other boy frowned with bitter scorn. "Teachers! Teachers don't order *me* around, I can tell you! They're mighty careful how they try to run over Rupe Collins."

"Who's Rupe Collins?"

"Who is he?" echoed the fat-faced boy incredulously. "Say, ain't you got *any* sense?"

"What?"

"Say, wouldn't you be just as happy if you had *some* sense?"

"Ye-es." Penrod's answer, like the look he lifted to the impressive stranger, was meek and placative. "Rupe Collins is the principal at your school, I guess."

The other yelled with jeering laughter, and mocked Penrod's manner and voice. "'Rupe Collins is the principal at your school, I guess!'" He laughed harshly again, then suddenly showed truculence. "Say, 'bo, whyn't you learn enough to go in the house when it rains? What's the matter of you, anyhow?"

"Well," urged Penrod timidly, "nobody ever *told* me who Rupe Collins is: I got a *right* to think he's the principal, haven't I?"

The fat-faced boy shook his head disgustedly. "Honest, you make me sick!"

Penrod's expression became one of despair. "Well, who *is* he?" he cried.

"'Who *is* he?'" mocked the other, with a scorn that withered. "'Who *is* he?' Me!"

"Oh!" Penrod was humiliated but relieved: he felt that he had proved himself criminally ignorant, yet a peril seemed to have passed. "Rupe Collins is *your* name, then, I guess. I kind of thought it was, all the time."

The fat-faced boy still appeared embittered, burlesquing this speech in a hateful falsetto. "'Rupe Collins is *your* name, then, I guess!' Oh, you 'kind of thought it was, all the time,' did you?" Suddenly concentrating his brow into a histrionic scowl he thrust his face within an inch of Penrod's. "Yes, sonny, Rupe Collins is my name, and you better look out what you say when he's around or you'll get in big trouble! *You understan' that, 'bo?*"

Penrod was cowed but fascinated: he felt that there was something dangerous and dashing about this newcomer.

"Yes," he said, feebly, drawing back. "My name's Penrod Schofield."

"Then I reckon your father and mother ain't got good sense," said Mr. Collins promptly, this also being formula.

"Why?"

" 'Cause if they had they'd of give you a good name!" And the agreeable youth instantly rewarded himself for the wit with another yell of rasping laughter, after which he pointed suddenly at Penrod's right hand.

"Where'd you get that wart on your finger?" he demanded severely.

" Yes, sonny, Rupe Collins is my name, and you better look out what you say when he's around! "

"Which finger?" asked the mystified Penrod, extending his hand.

"The middle one."

"Where?"

"There!" exclaimed Rupe Collins, seizing and vigorously twisting the wartless finger naïvely offered for his inspection.

"Quit!" shouted Penrod in agony. "*Quee*-yut!"

"Say your prayers!" commanded Rupe, and continued to twist the luckless finger until Penrod writhed to his knees.

"*Ow!*" The victim, released, looked grievously upon the still painful finger.

At this Rupe's scornful expression altered to one of contrition. "Well, I declare!" he exclaimed remorsefully. "I didn't s'pose it would hurt. Turn about's fair play; so now you do that to me."

He extended the middle finger of his left hand and Penrod promptly seized it, but did not twist it, for he was instantly swung round with his back to his amiable new acquaintance: Rupe's right hand operated upon the back of Penrod's slender neck; Rupe's knee tortured the small of Penrod's back.

"*Ow!*" Penrod bent far forward involuntarily and went to his knees again.

"Lick dirt," commanded Rupe, forcing the captive's face to the sidewalk; and the suffering Penrod completed this ceremony.

Mr. Collins evinced satisfaction by means of his horse laugh. "You'd last jest about one day up at the Third!" he said. "You'd come runnin' home, yellin' '*Mom*-muh, *mom*-muh,' before recess was over!"

"No, I wouldn't," Penrod protested rather weakly, dusting his knees.

"You would, too!"

"No, I w ——"

"Looky here," said the fat-faced boy, darkly, "what you mean, counterdicking me?"

He advanced a step and Penrod hastily qualified his contradiction.

"I mean, I don't *think* I would. I ——"

"You better look out!" Rupe moved closer, and unexpectedly grasped the back of Penrod's neck again. "Say, 'I *would* run home yellin' "*Mom*-muh!"'"

"Ow! I *would* run home yellin' 'Mom-muh.'"

"There!" said Rupe, giving the helpless nape a final squeeze. "That's the way we do up at the Third."

Penrod rubbed his neck and asked meekly:

"Can you do that to any boy up at the Third?"

"See here now," said Rupe, in the tone of one goaded beyond all endurance, "*you* say if I can! You better say it quick, or ——"

"I knew you could," Penrod interposed hastily, with the pathetic semblance of a laugh. "I only said that in fun."

"In 'fun'!" repeated Rupe stormily. "You better look out how you ——"

"Well, I *said* I wasn't in earnest!" Penrod retreated a few steps. "*I* knew you could, all the time. I expect *I* could do it to some of the boys up at the Third, myself. Couldn't I?"

"No, you couldn't."

"Well, there must be *some* boy up there that I could ——"

"No they ain't! You better ——"

"I expect not, then," said Penrod, quickly.

"You *better* 'expect not.' Didn't I tell you once you'd never get back alive if you ever tried to come up around the Third? You want me to *show* you how we do up there, 'bo?"

He began a slow and deadly advance, whereupon Penrod timidly offered a diversion:

"Say, Rupe, I got a box of rats in our stable under a glass cover, so you can watch 'em jump around when you hammer on the box. Come on and look at 'em."

"All right," said the fat-faced boy, slightly mollified. "We'll let Dan kill 'em."

"No, *sir!* I'm goin' to keep 'em. They're kind of pets; I've had 'em all summer — I got names for 'em, and ——"

"Looky here, 'bo. Did you hear me say we'll let Dan kill 'em?"

"Yes, but I won't ——"

"*What* won't you?" Rupe became sinister immediately. "It seems to me you're gettin' pretty fresh around here."

"Well, I don't want ——"

Mr. Collins once more brought into play the dreadful eye-to-eye scowl as practised "up at the Third," and, sometimes, also by young leading men upon the stage. Frowning appallingly, and thrusting forward his underlip, he placed his nose almost in contact with the nose of Penrod, whose eyes naturally became crossed.

"Dan kills the rats. See?" hissed the fat-faced boy, maintaining the horrible juxtaposition.

"Well, all right," said Penrod, swallowing. "*I* don't want 'em much." And when the pose had been relaxed, he stared at his new friend for a moment, almost with reverence. Then he brightened.

"Come on, Rupe!" he cried enthusiastically, as he climbed the fence. "We'll give our dogs a little live meat — 'bo!"

CHAPTER XXII

THE IMITATOR

AT THE dinner-table, that evening, Penrod surprised his family by remarking, in a voice they had never heard him attempt — a law-giving voice of intentional gruffness:

"Any man that's makin' a hunderd dollars a month is makin' good money."

"What?" asked Mr. Schofield, staring, for the previous conversation had concerned the illness of an infant relative in Council Bluffs.

"Any man that's makin' a hunderd dollars a month is makin' good money."

"What *is* he talking about!" Margaret appealed to the invisible.

"Well," said Penrod, frowning, "that's what foremen at the ladder works get."

"How in the world do you know?" asked his mother.

"Well, I *know* it! A hunderd dollars a month is good money, I tell you!"

"Well, what of it?" said the father, impatiently.

"Nothin'. I only said it was good money."

Mr. Schofield shook his head, dismissing the subject; and here he made a mistake: he should have followed up his son's singular contribution to the conversation. That would have revealed the fact that there was a certain Rupe Collins whose father was a foreman at the ladder works. All clues are important when a boy makes his first remark in a new key.

"'Good money'?" repeated Margaret, curiously. "What is 'good' money?"

Penrod turned upon her a stern glance. "Say, wouldn't you be just as happy if you had *some* sense?"

"Penrod!" shouted his father. But Penrod's mother gazed with dismay at her son: he had never before spoken like that to his sister.

Mrs. Schofield might have been more dismayed than she was, if she had realized that it was the beginning of an epoch. After dinner, Penrod was slightly scalded in the back as the result of telling Della, the cook, that there was a wart on the middle finger of her right hand. Della thus proving poor material for his new manner to work upon, he approached Duke, in the backyard, and, bending double, seized the lowly animal by the forepaws.

"I let you know my name's Penrod Schofield," hissed the boy. He protruded his underlip ferociously, scowled, and thrust forward his head until his nose touched the dog's. "And you better look out when Penrod Schofield's around, or you'll get in big trouble! *You understan' that, 'bo?*"

The next day, and the next, the increasing change in Penrod puzzled and distressed his family, who had no idea of its source. How might they guess that hero-worship takes such forms? They were vaguely conscious that a rather shabby boy, not of the neighbourhood, came to "play" with Penrod several times; but they failed to connect this circumstance with the peculiar behaviour of the son of the house, whose ideals (his father remarked) seemed to have suddenly become identical with those of Gyp the Blood.

Meanwhile, for Penrod himself, "life had taken on new meaning, new richness." He had become a fighting man — in conversation at least. "Do you want to know how I do when they try to slip up on me from behind?" he asked Della. And he enacted for her unappreciative eye a scene of fistic manœuvres wherein he held an imaginary antagonist helpless in a net of stratagems.

Frequently, when he was alone, he would outwit and pummel this same enemy, and, after a cunning feint, land a dolorous stroke full upon a face of air. "There! I guess you'll know better next time. That's the way we do up at the Third!"

Sometimes, in solitary pantomime, he encountered more than one opponent at a time, for numbers were apt to come upon him treacherously, especially at a little after his rising hour, when he might be caught at a disadvantage — perhaps standing on one leg to encase the other in his knickerbockers. Like lightning, he would hurl the trapping garment from him, and, ducking and pivoting, deal great sweeping blows among the circle of sneaking devils. (That was how he broke the clock in his bedroom.) And while these battles were occupying his attention, it was a waste of voice to call him to breakfast, though if his mother, losing patience, came to his room, she would find him seated on the bed pulling at a stocking. "Well, ain't I coming fast as I *can?*"

At the table and about the house generally he was bumptious, loud with fatuous misinformation, and assumed a domineering tone, which neither satire nor reproof seemed able to reduce; but it was among his own intimates that his new superiority was most outrageous. He twisted the fingers and squeezed the necks of all the boys of the neighbourhood, meeting their indignation with a hoarse and rasping laugh he had acquired after short practice in the stable, where he jeered and taunted the lawn-mower, the garden-scythe and the wheelbarrow quite out of countenance.

Likewise he bragged to the other boys by the hour, Rupe Collins being the chief subject of encomium — next to Penrod himself. "That's the way we do up at the Third," became staple explanation of violence, for Penrod, like Tartarin, was plastic in the hands of his own imagination, and at times convinced himself that he really was one of those dark and murderous spirits exclusively of whom "the Third" was composed — according to Rupe Collins.

Then, when Penrod had exhausted himself repeating to nausea accounts of the prowess of himself and his great friend, he would turn to two other subjects for vainglory. These were his father and Duke.

Mothers must accept the fact that between babyhood and manhood their sons do not boast of them. The boy, with boys, is a Choctaw; and either the influence or the protection of women is shameful. "Your mother won't let you," is an insult. But, "My father won't let me," is a dignified explanation and cannot be hooted. A boy is ruined among his fellows if he talks much of his mother or sisters; and he must recognize it as his duty to offer at least the appearance of persecution to all things ranked as female, such as cats and every species of fowl. But he must champion his father and his dog, and, ever ready to pit either against any challenger, must picture both as ravening for battle and absolutely unconquerable.

Penrod, of course, had always talked by the code, but, under the new stimulus, Duke was represented virtually as a cross between Bob, Son of Battle, and a South American vampire; and this in spite of the fact that Duke himself often sat close by, a living lie, with the hope of peace in his heart. As for

Penrod's father, that gladiator was painted as of sentiments and dimensions suitable to a super-demon composed of equal parts of Goliath, Jack Johnson and the Emperor Nero.

Even Penrod's walk was affected; he adopted a gait which was a kind of taunting swagger; and, when he passed other children on the street, he practised the habit of feinting a blow; then, as the victim dodged, he rasped out the triumphant horse laugh which he gradually mastered to horrible per-fection. He did this to Marjorie Jones — ay! this was their next meeting, and such is Eros, young! What was even worse, in Marjorie's opinion, he went on his way without explanation, and left her standing on the corner talking about it, long after he was out of hearing.

Within five days from his first encounter with Rupe Collins, Penrod had become unbearable. He even almost alienated Sam Williams, who for a time sub-mitted to finger twisting and neck squeezing and the new style of conversation, but finally declared that Penrod made him "sick." He made the statement with fervor, one sultry afternoon, in Mr. Schofield's stable, in the presence of Herman and Verman.

"You better look out, 'bo," said Penrod, threateningly. "I'll show you a little how we do up at the Third."

"Up at the Third!" Sam repeated with scorn. "You haven't ever been up there."

"I haven't?" cried Penrod. "I *haven't?*"

"No, you haven't!"

"Looky here!" Penrod, darkly argumentative, prepared to perform the eye-to-eye business. "When haven't I been up there?"

"You haven't *never* been up there!" In spite of Penrod's closely approaching nose Sam maintained his ground, and appealed for confirmation. "Has he, Herman?"

"I don' reckon so," said Herman, laughing.

"*What!*" Penrod transferred his nose to the immediate vicinity of Herman's nose. "You don't reckon so, 'bo, don't you? You better look out how you reckon around here! *You understan' that, 'bo?*"

Herman bore the eye-to-eye very well; indeed, it seemed to please him, for he continued to laugh, while Verman chuckled delightedly. The brothers had been in the country picking berries for a week, and it happened that this was their first experience of the new manifestation of Penrod.

"*Haven't* I been up at the Third?" the sinister Penrod demanded.

"I don' reckon so. How come you ast *me?*"

"Didn't you just hear me *say* I been up there?"

"Well," said Herman mischievously, "hearin' ain't believin'!"

Penrod clutched him by the back of the neck, but Herman, laughing loudly, ducked and released himself at once, retreating to the wall.

"You take that back!" Penrod shouted, striking out wildly.

"Don' git mad," begged the small darky, while a number of blows falling upon his warding arms failed to abate his amusement, and a sound one upon the cheek only made him laugh the more unrestrainedly. He behaved exactly as if Penrod were tickling him, and his brother, Verman, rolled with joy in a wheelbarrow. Penrod pummelled till he was tired, and produced no greater effect.

"There!" he panted, desisting finally. "*Now* I reckon you know whether I been up there or not!"

Herman rubbed his smitten cheek. "Pow!" he exclaimed. "Pow-ee! You cert'ny did lan' me good one *nat* time! Oo-ee! she *hurt!*"

"You'll get hurt worse'n that," Penrod assured

him, "if you stay around here much. Rupe Collins is comin' this afternoon, he said. We're goin' to make some policemen's billies out of the rake handle."

"You go' spoil new rake you' pa bought?"

"What do *we* care? I and Rupe got to have billies, haven't we?"

"How you make 'em?"

"Melt lead and pour in a hole we're goin' to make in the end of 'em. Then we're goin' to carry 'em in our pockets, and if anybody says anything to us — *oh*, oh! look out! They won't get a crack on the head — *oh*, no!"

"When's Rupe Collins coming?" Sam Williams inquired rather uneasily. He had heard a great deal too much of this personage, but as yet the pleasure of actual acquaintance had been denied him.

"He's liable to be here any time," answered Penrod. "You better look out. You'll be lucky if you get home alive, if you stay till *he* comes."

"I ain't afraid of him," Sam returned, conventionally.

"You are, too!" (There was some truth in the retort.) "There ain't any boy in this part of town but me that wouldn't be afraid of him. You'd be afraid to talk to him. You wouldn't get a word out of your mouth before old Rupie'd have you where you'd wished you never come around *him*, lettin' on like you was so much! *You* wouldn't run home yellin' 'Mom-muh' or nothin'! *Oh*, no!"

"Who Rupe Collins?" asked Herman.

"'Who Rupe Collins?'" Penrod mocked, and used his rasping laugh, but, instead of showing fright, Herman appeared to think he was meant to laugh, too; and so he did, echoed by Verman. "You just hang around here a little while longer," Penrod added, grimly, "and you'll find out who Rupe Collins is, and I pity *you* when you do!"

"What he go' do?"

"You'll see; that's all! You just wait and ——"

At this moment a brown hound ran into the stable through the alley door, wagged a greeting to Penrod, and fraternized with Duke. The fat-faced boy appeared upon the threshold and gazed coldly about the little company in the carriage-house, whereupon the coloured brethren, ceasing from merriment, were instantly impassive, and Sam Williams moved a little nearer the door leading into the yard.

Obviously, Sam regarded the newcomer as a redoubtable if not ominous figure. He was a head taller than either Sam or Penrod; head and shoulders taller than Herman, who was short for his age; and Verman could hardly be used for purposes of comparison at all, being a mere squat brown spot, not yet quite nine years on this planet. And to Sam's mind, the aspect of Mr. Collins realized Penrod's portentous foreshadowings. Upon the fat face there was an expression of truculent intolerance which had been cultivated by careful habit to such perfection that Sam's heart sank at sight of it. A somewhat enfeebled twin to this expression had of late often decorated the visage of Penrod, and appeared upon that ingenuous surface now, as he advanced to welcome the eminent visitor.

The host swaggered toward the door with a great deal of shoulder movement, carelessly feinting a slap at Verman in passing, and creating by various means the atmosphere of a man who has contemptuously amused himself with underlings while awaiting an equal.

"Hello, 'bo!" Penrod said in the deepest voice possible to him.

"Who you callin' 'bo?" was the ungracious response, accompanied by immediate action of a similar nature. Rupe held Penrod's head in the crook of an elbow and massaged his temples with a hard-pressing knuckle.

"I was only in fun, Rupie," pleaded the sufferer, and then, being set free, "Come here, Sam," he said.

"What for?"

Penrod laughed pityingly. "Pshaw, I ain't goin' to hurt you. Come on." Sam, maintaining his position near the other door, Penrod went to him and caught him round the neck.

"Watch me, Rupie!" Penrod called, and performed upon Sam the knuckle operation which he had himself just undergone, Sam submitting mechanically, his eyes fixed with increasing uneasiness upon Rupe Collins. Sam had a premonition that something even more painful than Penrod's knuckle was going to be inflicted upon him.

"*That* don' hurt," said Penrod, pushing him away.

"Yes, it does, too!" Sam rubbed his temple.

"Puh! It didn't hurt me, did it, Rupie? Come on in, Rupe: show this baby where he's got a wart on his finger."

"*You* showed me that trick," Sam objected. "You already did that to me. You tried it twice this afternoon and I don't know how many times before, only you weren't strong enough after the first time. Anyway, I know what it is, and I don't ——"

"Come on, Rupe," said Penrod. "Make the baby lick dirt."

At this bidding, Rupe approached, while Sam, still protesting, moved to the threshold of the outer door; but Penrod seized him by the shoulders and swung him indoors with a shout.

"Little baby wants to run home to its Mom-muh! Here he is, Rupie."

Thereupon was Penrod's treachery to an old comrade properly rewarded, for as the two struggled, Rupe caught each by the back of the neck, simultaneously, and, with creditable impartiality, forced both boys to their knees.

"Lick dirt!" he commanded, forcing them still forward, until their faces were close to the stable floor.

At this moment he received a real surprise. With a loud whack something struck the back of his head, and, turning, he beheld Verman in the act of lifting a piece of lath to strike again.

"Em moys ome!" said Verman, the Giant Killer.

"He tongue-tie'," Herman explained. "He say, let 'em boys alone."

Rupe addressed his host briefly:

"Chase them nigs out o' here!"

"Don' call me nig," said Herman.   "I mine my own biznuss.   You let 'em boys alone."

Rupe strode across the still prostrate Sam, stepped upon Penrod, and, equipping his countenance with the terrifying scowl and protruded jaw, lowered his head to the level of Herman's.

"Nig, you'll be lucky if you leave here alive!" And he leaned forward till his nose was within less than an inch of Herman's nose.

It could be felt that something awful was about to happen, and Penrod, as he rose from the floor, suffered an unexpected twinge of apprehension and remorse: he hoped that Rupe wouldn't *really* hurt Herman.   A sudden dislike of Rupe and Rupe's ways rose within him, as he looked at the big boy overwhelming the little darky with that ferocious scowl.   Penrod, all at once, felt sorry about something indefinable; and, with equal vagueness, he felt foolish.   "Come on, Rupe," he suggested, feebly, "let Herman go, and let's us make our billies out of the rake handle."

The rake handle, however, was not available, if Rupe had inclined to favour the suggestion.   Verman had discarded his lath for the rake, which he was at this moment lifting in the air.

"You ole black nigger," the fat-faced boy said venomously to Herman, "I'm agoin' to ——"

But he had allowed his nose to remain too long near Herman's. Penrod's familiar nose had been as close with only a ticklish spinal effect upon the not very remote descendant of Congo man-eaters. The result produced by the glare of Rupe's unfamiliar eyes, and by the dreadfully suggestive proximity of Rupe's unfamiliar nose, was altogether different. Herman's and Verman's Bangala great-grandfathers never considered people of their own jungle neighbourhood proper material for a meal, but they looked upon strangers — especially truculent strangers — as distinctly edible.

Penrod and Sam heard Rupe suddenly squawk and bellow; saw him writhe and twist and fling out his arms like flails, though without removing his face from its juxtaposition; indeed, for a moment, the two heads seemed even closer.

Then they separated — and battle was on!

CHAPTER XXIII

COLOURED TROOPS IN ACTION

HOW neat and pure is the task of the chronicler who has the tale to tell of a "good rousing fight" between boys or men who fight in the "good old English way," according to a model set for fights in books long before Tom Brown went to Rugby. There are seconds and rounds and rules of fair-play, and always there is great good feeling in the end — though sometimes, to vary the model, "the Butcher" defeats the hero — and the chronicler who stencils this fine old pattern on his page is certain of applause as the stirrer of "red blood." There is no surer recipe.

But when Herman and Verman set to't the record must be no more than a few fragments left by the expurgator. It has been perhaps sufficiently suggested that the altercation in Mr. Schofield's stable opened with mayhem in respect to the aggressor's nose. Expressing vocally his indignation and the extremity of his pained surprise, Mr. Collins stepped backward, holding his left hand over his nose, and striking at Herman with his right. Then Verman hit him with the rake.

Verman struck from behind. He struck as hard as he could. And he struck with the tines down. For, in his simple, direct African way he wished to kill his enemy, and he wished to kill him as soon as possible. That was his single, earnest purpose.

On this account, Rupe Collins was peculiarly unfortunate. He was plucky and he enjoyed conflict, but neither his ambitions nor his anticipations had ever included murder. He had not learned that an habitually aggressive person runs the danger of colliding with beings in one of those lower stages of evolution wherein theories about "hitting below the belt" have not yet made their appearance.

The rake glanced from the back of Rupe's head to

his shoulder, but it felled him.   Both darkies jumped full upon him instantly, and the three rolled and twisted upon the stable floor, unloosing upon the air sincere maledictions closely connected with complaints of cruel and unusual treatment; while certain expressions of feeling presently emanating from Herman and Verman indicated that Rupe Collins, in this extremity, was proving himself not too slavishly addicted to fighting by rule.   Dan and Duke, mistaking all for mirth, barked gayly.

From the panting, pounding, yelling heap issued words and phrases hitherto quite unknown to Penrod and Sam; also, a hoarse repetition in the voice of Rupe concerning his ear left it not to be doubted that additional mayhem was taking place.   Appalled, the two spectators retreated to the doorway nearest the yard, where they stood dumbly watching the cataclysm.

The struggle increased in primitive simplicity: time and again the howling Rupe got to his knees only to go down again as the earnest brothers, in their own way, assisted him to a more reclining position.   Primal forces operated here, and the two blanched, slightly higher products of evolution, Sam and Penrod, no more thought of interfering than they would have thought of interfering with an earthquake.

At last, out of the ruck rose Verman, disfigured and maniacal. With a wild eye he looked about him for his trusty rake; but Penrod, in horror, had long since thrown the rake out into the yard. Naturally, it had not seemed necessary to remove the lawn-mower.

The frantic eye of Verman fell upon the lawn-mower, and instantly he leaped to its handle. Shrilling a wordless war-cry, he charged, propelling the whirling, deafening knives straight upon the prone legs of Rupe Collins. The lawn-mower was sincerely intended to pass longitudinally over the body of Mr. Collins from heel to head; and it was the time for a death-song. Black Valkyrie hovered in the shrieking air.

"Cut his gizzud out!" shrieked Herman, urging on the whirling knives.

They touched and lacerated the shin of Rupe, as, with the supreme agony of effort a creature in mortal peril puts forth before succumbing, he tore himself free of Herman and got upon his feet.

Herman was up as quickly. He leaped to the wall and seized the garden-scythe that hung there.

"I'm go' to cut you' gizzud out," he announced definitely, "an' eat it!"

Rupe Collins had never run from anybody (except his father) in his life; he was not a coward; but the present situation was very, very unusual. He was already in a badly dismantled condition, and yet Herman and Verman seemed discontented with their work: Verman was swinging the grass-cutter about for a new charge, apparently still wishing to mow him, and Herman had made a quite plausible statement about what he intended to do with the scythe.

Rupe paused but for an extremely condensed survey of the horrible advance of the brothers, and then, uttering a blood-curdled scream of fear, ran out of the stable and up the alley at a speed he had never before attained, so that even Dan had hard work to keep within barking distance. And a 'cross-shoulder glance, at the corner, revealing Verman and Herman in pursuit, the latter waving his scythe overhead, Mr. Collins slackened not his gait, but, rather, out of great anguish, increased it; the while a rapidly developing purpose became firm in his mind — and ever after so remained — not only to refrain from visiting that neighbourhood again, but never by any chance to come within a mile of it.

From the alley door, Penrod and Sam watched the flight, and were without words. When the pursuit rounded the corner, the two looked wanly at each other, but neither spoke until the return of the brothers from the chase.

Herman and Verman came back, laughing and chuckling.

"Hiyi!" cackled Herman to Verman, as they came, "See 'at ole boy run!"

"Who-ee!" Verman shouted in ecstasy.

"Nev' did see boy run so fas'!" Herman continued, tossing the scythe into the wheelbarrow. "I bet he home in bed by viss time!"

Verman roared with delight, appearing to be wholly unconscious that the lids of his right eye were swollen shut and that his attire, not too finical before the struggle, now entitled him to unquestioned rank as a *sansculotte*. Herman was a similar ruin, and gave as little heed to his condition.

Penrod looked dazedly from Herman to Verman and back again. So did Sam Williams.

"Herman," said Penrod, in a weak voice, "you wouldn't *honest* of cut his gizzard out, would you?"

"Who? Me? I don' know. He mighty mean ole boy!" Herman shook his head gravely, and then, observing that Verman was again convulsed with unctuous merriment, joined laughter with his brother. "Sho! I guess I uz dess *talkin'* whens I said 'at! Reckon he thought I meant it, f'm de way he tuck an' run. Hiyi! Reckon he thought ole Herman bad man! No, suh, I uz dess talkin', 'cause I nev' would cut *no*body! I ain' tryin' git in no jail — *no*, suh!"

Penrod looked at the scythe; he looked at Herman. He looked at the lawn-mower, and he looked at Verman. Then he looked out in the yard at the rake. So did Sam Williams.

"Come on, Verman," said Herman. "We ain' got 'at stove-wood f' supper yit."

Giggling reminiscently, the brothers disappeared, leaving silence behind them in the carriage-house. Penrod and Sam retired slowly into the shadowy interior, each glancing, now and then, with a preoccupied air, at the open, empty doorway where the late afternoon sunshine was growing ruddy. At intervals one or the other scraped the floor reflectively with the side of his shoe. Finally, still without either having made any effort at conversation, they went out into the yard and stood, continuing their silence.

"Well," said Sam, at last, "I guess it's time I better be gettin' home.   So long, Penrod!"

"So long, Sam," said Penrod, feebly.

With a solemn gaze he watched his friend out of sight.   Then he went slowly into the house, and after an interval occupied in a unique manner, appeared in the library, holding a pair of brilliantly gleaming shoes in his hand.

Mr. Schofield, reading the evening paper, glanced frowningly over it at his offspring.

"Look, papa," said Penrod.   "I found your shoes where you'd taken 'em off in your room, to put on your slippers, and they were all dusty.   So I took 'em out on the back porch and gave 'em a good blacking.   They shine up fine, don't they?"

"Well, I'll be d-dud-dummed!" said the startled Mr. Schofield.

Penrod was zigzagging back to normal.

CHAPTER XXIV

"LITTLE GENTLEMAN"

THE midsummer sun was stinging hot outside the little barber-shop next to the corner drug store and Penrod, undergoing a toilette preliminary to his very slowly approaching twelfth birthday, was adhesive enough to retain upon his face much hair as it fell from the shears. There is a mystery here: the tonsorial processes are not un-agreeable to manhood; in truth, they are soothing; but the hairs detached from a boy's head get into his eyes, his ears, his nose, his mouth, and down his neck, and he does everywhere itch excrutiatingly.

Wherefore he blinks, winks, weeps, twitches, condenses his countenance, and squirms; and perchance the barber's scissors clip more than intended — belike an outlying flange of ear.

"Um—muh—*ow!*" said Penrod, this thing having happened.

"D' I touch y' up a little?" inquired the barber, smiling falsely.

"Ooh — *uh!*" The boy in the chair offered inarticulate protest, as the wound was rubbed with alum.

"*That* don't hurt!" said the barber. "You *will* get it, though, if you don't sit stiller," he continued, nipping in the bud any attempt on the part of his patient to think that he already had "it."

"Pfuff!" said Penrod, meaning no disrespect, but endeavouring to dislodge a temporary moustache from his lip.

"You ought to see how still that little Georgie Bassett sits," the barber went on, reprovingly. "I hear everybody says he's the best boy in town."

"Pfuff! *Phirr!*" There was a touch of intentional contempt in this.

"I haven't heard nobody around the neighbourhood makin' no such remarks," added the barber, "about nobody of the name of Penrod Schofield."

"Well," said Penrod, clearing his mouth after a struggle, "who wants 'em to? Ouch!"

"I hear they call Georgie Bassett the 'little gentleman,'" ventured the barber, provocatively, meeting with instant success.

"They better not call *me* that," returned Penrod truculently. "I'd like to hear anybody try. Just once, that's all! I bet they'd never try it ag—— *Ouch!*"

"Why? What'd you do to 'em?"

"It's all right what I'd *do!* I bet they wouldn't want to call me that again long as they lived!"

"What'd you do if it was a little girl? You wouldn't hit her, would you?"

"Well, I'd—— Ouch!"

"You wouldn't hit a little girl, would you?" the barber persisted, gathering into his powerful fingers a mop of hair from the top of Penrod's head and pulling that suffering head into an unnatural position. "Doesn't the Bible say it ain't never right to hit the weak sex?"

"Ow! *Say*, look *out!*"

"So you'd go and punch a pore, weak, little girl, would you?" said the barber, reprovingly.

"Well, who said I'd hit her?" demanded the

chivalrous Penrod. "I bet I'd *fix* her though, all right. She'd see!"

"You wouldn't call her names, would you?"

"No, I wouldn't! What hurt is it to call anybody names?"

"Is that *so!*" exclaimed the barber. "Then you was intending what I heard you hollering at Fisher's grocery delivery wagon driver fer a favour, the other day when I was goin' by your house, was you? I reckon I better tell him, because he says to me after*werds* if he ever lays eyes on you when you ain't in your own yard, he's goin' to do a whole lot o' things you ain't goin' to like! Yessir, that's what he says to *me!*"

"He better catch me first, I guess, before he talks so much."

"Well," resumed the barber, "that ain't sayin' what you'd do if a young lady ever walked up and called you a little gentleman. *I* want to hear what you'd do to her. I guess I know, though — come to think of it."

"What?" demanded Penrod.

"You'd sick that pore ole dog of yours on her cat, if she had one, I expect," guessed the barber derisively.

"No, I would not!"

"Well, what *would* you do?"

"I'd do enough.   Don't worry about that!"

"Well, suppose it was a boy, then: what'd you do if a boy come up to you and says, 'Hello, little gentleman'?"

"He'd be lucky," said Penrod, with a sinister frown, "if he got home alive."

"Suppose it was a boy twice your size?"

"Just let him try," said Penrod ominously. "You just let him try.   He'd never see daylight again; that's all!"

The barber dug ten active fingers into the helpless scalp before him and did his best to displace it, while the anguished Penrod, becoming instantly a seething crucible of emotion, misdirected his natural resentment into maddened brooding upon what he would do to a boy "twice his size" who should dare to call him "little gentleman."   The barber shook him as his father had never shaken him; the barber buffeted him, rocked him frantically to and fro; the barber seemed to be trying to wring his neck; and Penrod saw himself in staggering zigzag pictures, destroying large, screaming, fragmentary boys who had insulted him.

The torture stopped suddenly; and clenched, weeping eyes began to see again, while the barber applied cooling lotions which made Penrod smell like a coloured housemaid's ideal.

"Now what," asked the barber, combing the reeking locks gently, "what would it make you so mad fer, to have somebody call you a little gentle-man? It's a kind of compliment, as it were, you might say. What would you want to hit anybody fer *that* fer?"

To the mind of Penrod, this question was without meaning or reasonableness. It was within neither his power nor his desire to analyze the process by which the phrase had become offensive to him, and was now rapidly assuming the proportions of an outrage. He knew only that his gorge rose at the thought of it.

"You just let 'em try it!" he said threateningly, as he slid down from the chair. And as he went out of the door, after further conversation on the same subject, he called back those warning words once more: "Just let 'em try it! Just once — that's all *I* ask 'em to. They'll find out what they *get!*"

The barber chuckled. Then a fly lit on the bar-ber's nose and he slapped at it, and the slap missed the fly but did not miss the nose. The barber was irritated. At this moment his birdlike eye gleamed a gleam as it fell upon customers approaching: the prettiest little girl in the world, leading by the hand her baby brother, Mitchy-Mitch, coming to have Mitchy-Mitch's hair clipped, against the heat.

It was a hot day and idle, with little to feed the mind — and the barber was a mischievous man with an irritated nose. He did his worst.

Meanwhile, the brooding Penrod pursued his homeward way; no great distance, but long enough for several one-sided conflicts with malign insulters made of thin air. "You better *not* call me that!" he muttered. "You just try it, and you'll get what other people got when *they* tried it. You better not ack fresh with *me!* Oh, you *will*, will you?" He delivered a vicious kick full upon the shins of an iron fence-post, which suffered little, though Penrod instantly regretted his indiscretion. "Oof!" he grunted, hopping; and went on after bestowing a look of awful hostility upon the fence-post. "I guess you'll know better next time," he said, in parting, to this antagonist. "You just let me catch you around here again and I'll ——" His voice sank to inarticulate but ominous murmurings. He was in a dangerous mood.

Nearing home, however, his belligerent spirit was

diverted to happier interests by the discovery that some workmen had left a caldron of tar in the cross-street, close by his father's stable. He tested it, but found it inedible. Also, as a substitute for professional chewing-gum it was unsatisfactory, being insufficiently boiled down and too thin, though of a pleasant, lukewarm temperature. But it had an excess of one quality — it was sticky. It was the stickiest tar Penrod had ever used for any purposes whatsoever, and nothing upon which he wiped his hands served to rid them of it; neither his polka-dotted shirt waist nor his knickerbockers; neither the fence, nor even Duke, who came unthinkingly wagging out to greet him, and retired wiser.

Nevertheless, tar is tar. Much can be done with it, no matter what its condition; so Penrod lingered by the caldron, though from a neighbouring yard could be heard the voices of comrades, including that of Sam Williams. On the ground about the caldron were scattered chips and sticks and bits of wood to the number of a great multitude. Penrod mixed quantities of this refuse into the tar, and interested himself in seeing how much of it he could keep moving in slow swirls upon the ebon surface.

Other surprises were arranged for the absent

workmen. The caldron was almost full, and the surface of the tar near the rim. Penrod endeavoured to ascertain how many pebbles and brickbats, dropped in, would cause an overflow. Labouring heartily to this end, he had almost accomplished it, when he received the suggestion for an experiment on a much larger scale. Embedded at the corner of a grass-plot across the street was a whitewashed stone, the size of a small watermelon and serving no purpose whatever save the questionable one of decoration. It was easily pried up with a stick; though getting it to the caldron tested the full strength of the ardent labourer. Instructed to perform such a task, he would have sincerely maintained its impossibility; but now, as it was unbidden, and promised rather destructive results, he set about it with unconquerable energy, feeling certain that he would be rewarded with a mighty splash. Perspiring, grunting vehemently, his back aching and all muscles strained, he progressed in short stages until the big stone lay at the base of the caldron. He rested a moment, panting, then lifted the stone, and was bending his shoulders for the heave that would lift it over the rim, when a sweet, taunting voice, close behind him, startled him cruelly.

"How do you do, *little gentleman!*"

Penrod squawked, dropped the stone, and shouted, "Shut up, you dern fool!" purely from instinct, even before his about-face made him aware who had so spitefully addressed him.

It was Marjorie Jones. Always dainty, and prettily dressed, she was in speckless and starchy white to-day, and a refreshing picture she made, with the new-shorn and powerfully scented Mitchy-Mitch clinging to her hand. They had stolen up behind the toiler, and now stood laughing together in sweet merriment. Since the passing of Penrod's Rupe Collins period he had experienced some severe qualms at the recollection of his last meeting with Marjorie and his Apache behaviour; in truth, his heart instantly became as wax at sight of her, and he would have offered her fair speech; but, alas! in Marjorie's wonderful eyes there shone a consciousness of new powers for his undoing, and she denied him opportunity.

"Oh, *oh!*" she cried, mocking his pained outcry. "What a way for a *little gentleman* to talk! Little gentlemen don't say wicked ——"

"Marjorie!" Penrod, enraged and dismayed, felt himself stung beyond all endurance. Insult from her was bitterer to endure than from any other. "Don't you call me that again!"

"Why not, *little gentleman?*"

He stamped his foot. "You better stop!"

Marjorie sent into his furious face her lovely, spiteful laughter.

"Little gentleman, little gentleman, little gentleman!" she said deliberately. "How's the little gentleman, this afternoon? Hello, little gentleman!'

Penrod, quite beside himself, danced eccentrically. "Dry up!" he howled. "Dry up, dry up, dry up, dry *up!*"

Mitchy-Mitch shouted with delight and applied a finger to the side of the caldron — a finger immediately snatched away and wiped upon a handkerchief by his fastidious sister.

" 'Ittle gellamun!" said Mitchy-Mitch.

"You better look out!" Penrod whirled upon this small offender with grim satisfaction. Here was at least something male that could without dishonour be held responsible. "You say that again, and I'll give you the worst ——"

"You will *not!*" snapped Marjorie, instantly vitriolic. "He'll say just whatever he wants to, and he'll say it just as *much* as he wants to. Say it again, Mitchy-Mitch!"

"'Ittle gellamun!" said Mitchy-Mitch promptly.

"Ow-*yah!*" Penrod's tone-production was becoming affected by his mental condition. "You say that again, and I'll ——"

"Go on, Mitchy-Mitch," cried Marjorie. "He can't do a thing. He don't *dare!* Say it some more, Mitchy-Mitch — say it a whole lot!"

Mitchy-Mitch, his small, fat face shining with confidence in his immunity, complied.

"'Ittle gellamun!" he squeaked malevolently. "'Ittle gellamun! 'Ittle gellamun! 'Ittle gellamun!"

The desperate Penrod bent over the whitewashed rock, lifted it, and then — outdoing Porthos, John Ridd, and Ursus in one miraculous burst of strength — heaved it into the air.

Marjorie screamed.

But it was too late. The big stone descended into the precise midst of the caldron and Penrod got his mighty splash. It was far, far beyond his expectations.

Spontaneously there were grand and awful effects — volcanic spectacles of nightmare and eruption.

A black sheet of eccentric shape rose out of the caldron and descended upon the three children, who had no time to evade it.

After it fell, Mitchy-Mitch, who stood nearest the caldron, was the thickest, though there was enough for all. Bre'r Rabbit would have fled from any of them.

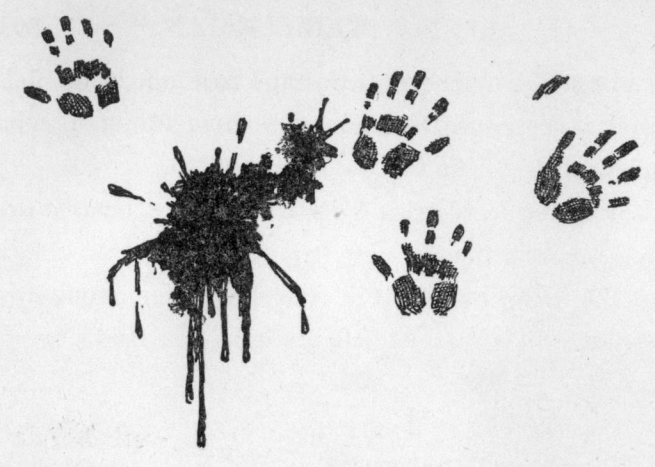

CHAPTER XXV

TAR

WHEN Marjorie and Mitchy-Mitch got their breath, they used it vocally; and seldom have more penetrating sounds issued from human throats. Coincidentally, Marjorie, quite baresark, laid hands upon the largest stick within reach and fell upon Penrod with blind fury. He had the presence of mind to flee, and they went round and round the caldron, while Mitchy-Mitch feebly endeavoured to follow — his appearance, in this pursuit, being pathetically like that of a bug fished out of an ink-well, alive but discouraged.

Attracted by the riot, Samuel Williams made his appearance, vaulting a fence, and was immediately followed by Maurice Levy and Georgie Bassett. They stared incredulously at the extraordinary spectacle before them.

"Little GEN-TIL-MUN!" shrieked Marjorie, with a wild stroke that landed full upon Penrod's tarry cap.

"*Ooach!*" bleated Penrod.

"It's Penrod!" shouted Sam Williams, recognizing him by the voice. For an instant he had been in some doubt.

"Penrod Schofield!" exclaimed Georgie Bassett. "*What* does this mean?" That was Georgie's style, and had helped to win him his title.

Marjorie leaned, panting, upon her stick. "I cu-called — uh — him — oh!" she sobbed — "I called him a lul-little — oh — gentlcman! And ob — lul-look! — oh! lul-look at my du-dress! Lul-look at Mumitchy — oh — Mitch — oh!"

Unexpectedly, she smote again — with results — and then, seizing the indistinguishable hand of Mitchy-Mitch, she ran wailing homeward down the street.

" 'Little gentleman?' " said Georgie Bassett, with

some evidences of disturbed complacency. "Why, that's what they call *me!*"

"Yes, and you *are* one, too!" shouted the maddened Penrod. "But you better not let anybody call *me* that! I've stood enough around here for one day, and you can't run over *me*, Georgie Bassett. Just you put that in your gizzard and smoke it!"

"Anybody has a perfect right," said Georgie, with dignity, "to call a person a little gentleman. There's lots of names nobody ought to call, but this one's a *nice* ——"

"You better look out!"

Unavenged bruises were distributed all over Penrod, both upon his body and upon his spirit. Driven by subtle forces, he had dipped his hands in catastrophe and disaster: it was not for a Georgie Bassett to beard him. Penrod was about to run amuck.

"I haven't called you a little gentleman, yet," said Georgie. "I only said it. Anybody's got a right to *say* it."

"Not around *me!* You just try it again and ——"

"I shall say it," returned Georgie, "all I please. Anybody in this town has a right to *say* 'little gentleman' ——"

Bellowing insanely, Penrod plunged his right hand

into the caldron, rushed upon Georgie and made awful work of his hair and features.

Alas, it was but the beginning! Sam Williams and Maurice Levy screamed with delight, and, simultaneously infected, danced about the struggling pair, shouting frantically:

"Little gentleman! Little gentleman! Sick him, Georgie! Sick him, little gentleman! Little gentleman! Little gentleman!"

The infuriated outlaw turned upon them with blows and more tar, which gave Georgie Bassett his opportunity and later seriously impaired the purity of his fame. Feeling himself hopelessly tarred, he dipped both hands repeatedly into the caldron and applied his gatherings to Penrod. It was bringing coals to Newcastle, but it helped to assuage the just wrath of Georgie.

The four boys gave a fine imitation of the Laocoön group complicated by an extra figure — frantic splutterings and chokings, strange cries and stranger words issued from this tangle; hands dipped lavishly into the inexhaustible reservoir of tar, with more and more picturesque results. The caldron had been elevated upon bricks and was not perfectly balanced; and under a heavy impact of the struggling group it lurched and went partly over, pouring forth a Stygian tide which formed a deep pool in the gutter.

It was the fate of Master Roderick Bitts, that exclusive and immaculate person, to make his appearance upon the chaotic scene at this juncture. All in the cool of a white "sailor suit," he turned aside from the path of duty — which led straight to the house of a maiden aunt — and paused to hop with joy upon the sidewalk. A repeated epithet. continuously half panted, half squawked, somewhere in the nest of gladiators, caught his ear, and he took it up excitedly, not knowing why.

"Little gentleman!" shouted Roderick, jumping up and down in childish glee. "Little gentleman! Little gentleman! Lit ——"

A frightful figure tore itself free from the group, encircled this innocent bystander with a black arm, and hurled him headlong. Full length and flat on his face went Roderick into the Stygian pool. The frightful figure was Penrod. Instantly, the pack flung themselves upon him again, and, carrying them with him, he went over upon Roderick, who from that instant was as active a belligerent as any there.

Thus began the Great Tar Fight, the origin of which proved, afterward, so difficult for parents to

Thus began the Great Tar Fight

trace, owing to the opposing accounts of the combatants. Marjorie said Penrod began it; Penrod said Mitchy-Mitch began it; Sam Williams said Georgie Bassett began it; Georgie and Maurice Levy said Penrod began it; Roderick Bitts, who had not recognized his first assailant, said Sam Williams began it.

Nobody thought of accusing the barber. But the barber did not begin it; it was the fly on the barber's nose that began it — though, of course, something else began the fly. Somehow, we never manage to hang the real offender.

The end came only with the arrival of Penrod's mother, who had been having a painful conversation by telephone with Mrs. Jones, the mother of Marjorie, and came forth to seek an errant son. It is a mystery how she was able to pick out her own, for by the time she got there his voice was too hoarse to be recognizable.

Mr. Schofield's version of things was that Penrod was insane. "He's a stark, raving lunatic!" declared the father, descending to the library from a before-dinner interview with the outlaw, that evening. "I'd send him to military school, but I don't believe they'd take him. Do you know *why* he says all that awfulness happened?"

"When Margaret and I were trying to scrub him," responded Mrs. Schofield wearily, "he said 'everybody' had been calling him names."

" 'Names!' " snorted her husband. " 'Little gentleman!' *That's* the vile epithet they called him! And because of it he wrecks the peace of six homes!"

"*Sh!* Yes; he told us about it," said Mrs. Schofield, moaning. "He told us several hundred times, I should guess, though I didn't count. He's got it fixed in his head, and we couldn't get it out. All we could do was to put him in the closet. He'd have gone out again after those boys if we hadn't. I don't know *what* to make of him!"

"He's a mystery to *me!*" said her husband. "And he refuses to explain why he objects to being called 'little gentleman.' Says he'd do the same thing — and worse — if anybody dared to call him that again. He said if the President of the United States called him that he'd try to whip him. How long did you have him locked up in the closet?"

"*Sh!*" said Mrs. Schofield warningly. "About two hours; but I don't think it softened his spirit at all, because when I took him to the barber's to get his hair clipped again, on account of the tar in it,

Sammy Williams and Maurice Levy were there for
the same reason, and they just *whispered* 'little
gentleman,' so low you could hardly hear them —
and Penrod began fighting with them right before
me, and it was really all the barber and I could do to
drag him away from them. The barber was very
kind about it, but Penrod ——"

"I tell you he's a lunatic!" Mr. Schofield would
have said the same thing of a Frenchman infuriated
by the epithet "camel." The philosophy of insult
needs expounding.

"*Sh!*" said Mrs. Schofield. "It does seem a kind
of frenzy."

"Why on earth should any sane person mind
being called ——"

"*Sh!*" said Mrs. Schofield. "It's beyond *me!*"

"What are you *sh*-ing me for?" demanded Mr.
Schofield explosively.

"*Sh!*" said Mrs. Schofield. "It's Mr. Kinosling,
the new rector of Saint Joseph's."

"Where?"

"*Sh!*" On the front porch with Margaret; he's
going to stay for dinner. I do hope ——"

"Bachelor, isn't he?"

"Yes."

"*Our* old minister was speaking of him the other day," said Mr. Schofield, "and he didn't seem so terribly impressed."

"*Sh!* Yes; about thirty, and of course *so* superior to most of Margaret's friends — boys home from college. She thinks she likes young Robert Williams, I know — but he laughs so much! Of course there isn't any comparison. Mr. Kinosling talks so intellectually; it's a good thing for Margaret to hear that kind of thing, for a change — and, of course, he's very spiritual. He seems very much interested in her." She paused to muse. "I think Margaret likes him; he's so different, too. It's the third time he's dropped in this week, and I ——"

"Well," said Mr. Schofield grimly, "if you and Margaret want him to come again, you'd better not let him see Penrod."

"But he's asked to see him; he seems interested in meeting all the family. And Penrod nearly always behaves fairly well at table." She paused, and then put to her husband a question referring to his interview with Penrod upstairs. "Did you — did you — do it?"

"No," he answered gloomily. "No, I didn't, but ——" He was interrupted by a violent crash of china and metal in the kitchen, a shriek from Della, and the outrageous voice of Penrod. The well-informed Della, ill-inspired to set up for a wit, had ventured to address the scion of the house roguishly as 'little gentleman,' and Penrod, by means of the rapid elevation of his right foot, had removed from her supporting hands a laden tray. Both parents started for the kitchen, Mr. Schofield completing his interrupted sentence on the way.

"But I will, now!"

The rite thus promised was hastily but accurately performed in that apartment most distant from the front porch; and, twenty minutes later, Penrod descended to dinner. The Rev. Mr. Kinosling had asked for the pleasure of meeting him, and it had been decided that the only course possible was to cover up the scandal for the present, and to offer an undisturbed and smiling family surface to the gaze of the visitor.

Scorched but not bowed, the smouldering Penrod was led forward for the social formulæ simultaneously with the somewhat bleak departure of Robert Williams, who took his guitar with him, this time, and went in forlorn unconsciousness of the powerful forces already set in secret motion to be his allies.

The punishment just undergone had but made the haughty and unyielding soul of Penrod more stalwart in revolt; he was unconquered. Every time the one intolerable insult had been offered him, his resentment had become the hotter, his vengeance the more instant and furious. And, still burning with outrage, but upheld by the conviction of right, he was determined to continue to the last drop of his blood the defense of his honour, whenever it should be assailed, no matter how mighty or august the powers that attacked it. In all ways, he was a very sore boy.

During the brief ceremony of presentation, his usually inscrutable countenance wore an expression interpreted by his father as one of insane obstinacy, while Mrs. Schofield found it an incentive to inward prayer. The fine graciousness of Mr. Kinosling, however, was unimpaired by the glare of virulent suspicion given him by this little brother: Mr. Kinosling mistook it for a natural curiosity concerning one who might possibly become, in time, a member of the family. He patted Penrod upon the head, which was, for many reasons, in no condition to be patted with any pleasure to the pattee. Penrod felt himself in the presence of a new enemy.

"How do you do, my little lad," said Mr. Kinosling. "I trust we shall become fast friends."

To the ear of his little lad, it seemed he said, "A trost we shall bick-home fawst frainds." Mr. Kinosling's pronunciation was, in fact, slightly precious; and the little lad, simply mistaking it for some cryptic form of mockery of himself, assumed a manner and expression which argued so ill for the proposed friendship that Mrs. Schofield hastily interposed the suggestion of dinner, and the small procession went in to the dining-room.

"It has been a delicious day," said Mr. Kinosling, presently; "warm but balmy." With a benevolent smile he addressed Penrod, who sat opposite him. "I suppose, little gentleman, you have been indulging in the usual outdoor sports of vacation?"

Penrod laid down his fork and glared, open-mouthed at Mr. Kinosling.

"You'll have another slice of breast of the chicken?" Mr. Schofield inquired, loudly and quickly.

"A lovely day!" exclaimed Margaret, with equal promptitude and emphasis. "Lovely, oh, lovely! Lovely!"

"Beautiful, beautiful, beautiful!" said Mrs. Schofield, and after a glance at Penrod which confirmed her impression that he intended to say something, she continued, "Yes, beautiful, beautiful, beautiful, beautiful, beautiful beautiful!"

Penrod closed his mouth and sank back in his chair — and his relatives took breath.

Mr. Kinosling looked pleased. This responsive family, with its ready enthusiasm, made the kind of audience he liked. He passed a delicate white hand gracefully over his tall, pale forehead, and smiled indulgently.

"Youth relaxes in summer," he said. "Boyhood is the age of relaxation; one is playful, light, free, unfettered. One runs and leaps and enjoys one's self with one's companions. It is good for the little lads to play with their friends; they jostle, push, and wrestle, and simulate little, happy struggles with one another in harmless conflict. The young muscles are toughening. It is good. Boyish chivalry develops, enlarges, expands. The young learn quickly, intuitively, spontaneously. They perceive the obligations of *noblesse oblige*. They begin to comprehend the necessity of caste and its requirements. They learn what birth means — ah, — that is, they learn what it means to be well born. They learn courtesy in their games; they learn politeness, consideration for one another in their pastimes, amusements, lighter occupations. I make it my pleasure to join them often, for I sympathize with them in all their wholesome joys as well as in their little bothers and perplexities. I understand them, you see; and let me tell you it is no easy matter to understand the little lads and lassies." He sent to each listener his beaming glance, and, permitting it to come to rest upon Penrod, inquired:

"And what do you say to that, little gentleman?"

Mr. Schofield uttered a stentorian cough. "More? You'd better have some more chicken! More! Do!"

"More chicken!" urged Margaret simultaneously. "Do please! Please! More! Do! More!"

"Beautiful, beautiful," began Mrs. Schofield. "Beautiful, beautiful, beautiful, beautiful ——"

It is not known in what light Mr. Kinosling viewed the expression of Penrod's face. Perhaps he mistook it for awe; perhaps he received no impression at all of its extraordinary quality. He was a rather self-engrossed young man, just then engaged in a double occupation, for he not only talked, but supplied from his own consciousness a critical though favourable auditor as well, which of course kept him quite busy. Besides, it is oftener than is suspected

the case that extremely peculiar expressions upon
the countenances of boys are entirely overlooked,
and suggest nothing to the minds of people staring
straight at them. Certainly Penrod's expression —
which, to the perception of his family, was perfectly
horrible — caused not the faintest perturbation in
the breast of Mr. Kinosling.

Mr. Kinosling waived the chicken, and continued
to talk. "Yes, I think I may claim to understand
boys," he said, smiling thoughtfully. "One has
been a boy one's self. Ah, it is not all playtime! I
hope our young scholar here does not overwork
himself at his Latin, at his classics, as I did, so that
at the age of eight years I was compelled to wear
glasses. He must be careful not to strain the little
eyes at his scholar's tasks, not to let the little shoulders grow round over his scholar's desk. Youth is
golden; we should keep it golden, bright, glistening.
Youth should frolic, should be sprightly; it should
play its cricket, its tennis, its hand-ball. It should
run and leap; it should laugh, should sing madrigals
and glees, carol with the lark, ring out in chanties,
folk-songs, ballads, roundelays ——"

He talked on. At any instant Mr. Schofield held
himself ready to cough vehemently and shout, "More

chicken," to drown out Penrod in case the fatal words again fell from those eloquent lips; and Mrs. Schofield and Margaret kept themselves prepared at all times to assist him. So passed a threatening meal, which Mrs. Schofield hurried, by every means within decency, to its conclusion. She felt that somehow they would all be safer out in the dark of the front porch, and led the way thither as soon as possible.

"No cigar, I thank you." Mr. Kinosling, establishing himself in a wicker chair beside Margaret, waved away her father's proffer. "I do not smoke. I have never tasted tobacco in any form." Mrs. Schofield was confirmed in her opinion that this would be an ideal son-in-law. Mr. Schofield was not so sure.

"No," said Mr. Kinosling. "No tobacco for me. No cigar, no pipe, no cigarette, no cheroot. For me, a book — a volume of poems, perhaps. Verses, rhymes, lines metrical and cadenced — those are my dissipation. Tennyson by preference: 'Maud,' or 'Idylls of the King' — poetry of the sound Victorian days; there is none later. Or Longfellow will rest me in a tired hour. Yes; for me, a book, a volume in the hand, held lightly between the fingers."

Mr. Kinosling looked pleasantly at his fingers as

he spoke, waving his hand in a curving gesture which brought it into the light of a window faintly illumined from the interior of the house. Then he passed those graceful fingers over his hair, and turned toward Penrod, who was perched upon the railing in a dark corner.

"The evening is touched with a slight coolness," said Mr. Kinosling. "Perhaps I may request the little gentleman ——"

"*B'gr-r-ruff!*" coughed Mr. Schofield. "You'd better change your mind about a cigar."

"No, I thank you. I was about to request the lit ——"

"*Do* try one," Margaret urged. "I'm sure papa's are nice ones. Do try ——"

"No, I thank you. I remarked a slight coolness in the air, and my hat is in the hallway. I was about to request ——"

"I'll get it for you," said Penrod suddenly.

"If you will be so good," said Mr. Kinosling. "It is a black bowler hat, little gentleman, and placed upon a table in the hall."

"I know where it is." Penrod entered the door, and a feeling of relief, mutually experienced, carried from one to another of his three relatives their interchanged congratulations that he had recovered his sanity.

" 'The day is done, and the darkness,' " began Mr. Kinosling — and recited that poem entire. He followed it with "The Children's Hour," and after a pause at the close, to allow his listeners time for a little reflection upon his rendition, he passed his hand again over his head, and called, in the direction of the doorway:

"I believe I will take my hat now, little gentleman."

"Here it is," said Penrod, unexpectedly climbing over the porch railing, in the other direction. His mother and father and Margaret had supposed him to be standing in the hallway out of deference, and because he thought it tactful not to interrupt the recitations. All of them remembered, later, that this supposed thoughtfulness on his part struck them as unnatural.

"Very good, little gentleman!" said Mr. Kinosling, and being somewhat chilled, placed the hat firmly upon his head, pulling it down as far as it would go. It had a pleasant warmth, which he noticed at once. The next instant, he noticed something else, a peculiar sensation of the scalp — a sensation which he was quite unable to define. He lifted his hand to take the hat off, and entered upon a strange experience: his hat seemed to have decided to remain where it was.

"Do you like Tennyson as much as Longfellow, Mr. Kinosling?" inquired Margaret.

"I — ah — I cannot say," he returned absently. "I — ah — each has his own — ugh! flavour and savour, each his — ah — ah ——"

Struck by a strangeness in his tone, she peered at him curiously through the dusk. His outlines were indistinct, but she made out that his arms were uplifted in a singular gesture. He seemed to be wrenching at his head.

"Is — is anything the matter?" she asked anxiously. "Mr. Kinosling, are you ill?"

"Not at — ugh! — all," he replied, in the same odd tone. "I — ah — I believe — *ugh!*"

He dropped his hands from his hat, and rose. His manner was slightly agitated. "I fear I may have taken a trifling — ah — cold. I should — ah — perhaps be — ah — better at home. I will — ah — say good-night."

At the steps, he instinctively lifted his hand to remove his hat, but did not do so, and, saying "Goodnight," again in a frigid voice, departed with visible stiffness from that house, to return no more.

"Well, of all——!" cried Mrs. Schofield, astounded. "What was the matter? He just went — like that!" She made a flurried gesture. "In heaven's name, Margaret, what *did* you say to him?"

"*I!*" exclaimed Margaret indignantly. "Nothing! He just *went!*"

"Why, he didn't even take off his hat when he said good-night!" said Mrs. Schofield.

Margaret, who had crossed to the doorway, caught the ghost of a whisper behind her, where stood Penrod.

"*You bet he didn't!*"

He knew not that he was overheard.

A frightful suspicion flashed through Margaret's mind — a suspicion that Mr. Kinosling's hat would have to be either boiled off or shaved off. With growing horror she recalled Penrod's long absence when he went to bring the hat.

"Penrod," she cried, "let me see your hands!"

She had toiled at those hands herself late that afternoon, nearly scalding her own, but at last achieving a lily purity.

"Let me see your hands!"

She seized them.

Again they were tarred!

CHAPTER XXVI

THE QUIET AFTERNOON

PERHAPS middle-aged people might discern Nature's real intentions in the matter of pain if they would examine a boy's punishments and sorrows, for he prolongs neither beyond their actual duration. With a boy, trouble must be of Homeric dimensions to last overnight. To him, every next day is really a new day. Thus, Penrod woke, next morning, with neither the unspared rod, nor Mr. Kinosling in his mind. Tar, itself, so far as his consideration of it went, might have been an undiscovered substance. His mood was cheerful and mercantile; some process having worked mysteriously within him, during the night, to the result that his first waking thought was of profits connected with the sale of old iron — or perhaps a ragman had passed the house, just before he woke.

By ten o'clock he had formed a partnership with the indeed amiable Sam, and the firm of Schofield and Williams plunged headlong into commerce. Heavy dealings in rags, paper, old iron and lead gave the firm a balance of twenty-two cents on the evening of the third day; but a venture in glassware, following, proved disappointing on account of the scepticism of all the druggists in that part of town, even after seven laborious hours had been spent in cleansing a wheelbarrow-load of old medicine bottles with hydrant water and ashes. Likewise, the partners were disheartened by their failure to dispose of a crop of "greens," although they had uprooted specimens of that decorative and unappreciated flower, the dandelion, with such persistence and energy that the Schofields' and Williams' lawns looked curiously haggard for the rest of that summer.

The fit passed: business languished; became extinct. The dog-days had set in.

One August afternoon was so hot that even boys

sought indoor shade.   In the dimness of the vacant
carriage-house of the stable, lounged Masters Penrod
Schofield, Samuel Williams, Maurice Levy, Georgie
Bassett, and Herman.   They sat still and talked.   It is
a hot day, in rare truth, when boys devote themselves
principally to conversation, and this day was that hot.

Their elders should beware such days.   Peril
hovers near when the fierceness of weather forces
inaction and boys in groups are quiet.   The more
closely volcanoes, Western rivers, nitroglycerin, and
boys are pent, the deadlier is their action at the
point of outbreak.   Thus, parents and guardians
should look for outrages of the most singular violence
and of the most peculiar nature during the confining
weather of February and August.

The thing which befell upon this broiling afternoon
began to brew and stew peacefully enough.   All was
innocence and languor; no one could have foretold
the eruption.

They were upon their great theme: "When I
get to be a man!" Being human, though boys, they
considered their present estate too commonplace
to be dwelt upon.   So, when the old men gather,
they say: "When I was a boy!"   It really is the
land of nowadays that we never discover.

"When I'm a man," said Sam Williams, "I'm goin' to hire me a couple of coloured waiters to swing me in a hammock and keep pourin' ice-water on me all day out o' those waterin'-cans they sprinkle flowers from. I'll hire you for one of 'em, Herman."

"No; you ain' goin' to," said Herman promptly. "You ain' no flowuh. But nev' min' nat, anyway. Ain' nobody goin' hiah me whens I'm a man. Goin' be my own boss. I'm go' be a rai'road man!"

"You mean like a superintendent, or sumpthing like that, and sell tickets?" asked Penrod.

"Sup'in — nev' min' nat! Sell ticket? No suh! Go' be a po'tuh! My uncle a po'tuh right now. Solid gole buttons — oh, oh!"

"Generals get a lot more buttons than porters," said Penrod. "Generals ——"

"Po'tuhs make the bes' livin'," Herman interrupted. "My uncle spen' mo' money 'n any white man n'is town."

"Well, I rather be a general," said Penrod, "or a senator, or sumpthing like that."

"Senators live in Warshington," Maurice Levy contributed the information. "I been there. Warshington ain't so much; Niag'ra Falls is a hunderd times as good as Warshington. So's 'Tlantic City.

I was there, too. I been everywhere there is.
I ——"

"Well, anyway," said Sam Williams, raising his
voice in order to obtain the floor, "anyway, I'm
goin' to lay in a hammock all day, and have ice-
water sprinkled on top o' me, and I'm goin' to lay
there all night, too, and the next day. I'm goin'
to lay there a couple o' years, maybe."

"I bet you don't!" exclaimed Maurice. "What'd
you do in winter?"

"What?"

"What you goin' to do when it's winter, out in a
hammock with water sprinkled on top o' you all
day? I bet you ——"

"I'd stay right there," Sam declared, with strong
conviction, blinking as he looked out through the
open doors at the dazzling lawn and trees, trembling
in the heat. "They couldn't sprinkle too much for
me!"

"It'd make icicles all over you, and ——"

"I wish it would," said Sam. "I'd eat 'em up."

"And it'd snow on you ——"

"Yay! I'd swaller it as fast as it'd come down.
I wish I had a *barrel* o' snow right now. I wish this
whole barn was full of it. I wish they wasn't

anything in the whole world except just good ole snow."

Penrod and Herman rose and went out to the hydrant, where they drank long and ardently. Sam was still talking about snow when they returned.

"No, I wouldn't just roll in it. I'd stick it all round inside my clo'es, and fill my hat. No, I'd freeze a big pile of it all hard, and I'd roll her out flat and then I'd carry her down to some ole tailor's and have him make me a *suit* out of her, and ——"

"Can't you keep still about your ole snow?" demanded Penrod petulantly. "Makes me so thirsty I can't keep still, and I've drunk so much now I bet I bust. That ole hydrant water's mighty near hot, anyway."

"I'm goin' to have a big store, when I grow up," volunteered Maurice.

"Candy store?" asked Penrod.

"*No*, sir! I'll have candy in it, but not to eat, so much. It's goin' to be a deportment store: ladies' clothes, gentlemen's clothes, neckties, china goods, leather goods, nice lines in woollings and lace goods ——"

"Yay! I wouldn't give a five-for-a-cent marble for your whole store," said Sam. "Would you, Penrod?"

"Not for ten of 'em; not for a million of 'em!   *I*'m goin' to have ——"

"Wait!" clamoured Maurice.   "You'd be foolish, because they'd be a toy deportment in my store where they'd be a hunderd marbles!   So, how much would you think your five-for-a-cent marble counts for? And when I'm keepin' my store I'm goin' to get married."

"Yay!" shrieked Sam derisively.   "*Married!* Listen!"   Penrod and Herman joined in the howl of contempt.

"Certumly I'll get married," asserted Maurice stoutly. "I'll get married to Marjorie Jones. She likes me awful good, and I'm her beau."

"What makes you think so?" inquired Penrod in a cryptic voice.

"Because she's my beau, too," came the prompt answer.   "I'm her beau because she's my beau; I guess that's plenty reason!   I'll get married to her as soon as I get my store running nice."

Penrod looked upon him darkly, but, for the moment, held his peace.

"Married!" jeered Sam Williams.   "Married to Marjorie Jones!   You're the only boy I ever heard say he was going to get married.   I wouldn't get married for — why, I wouldn't for — for ——"

Unable to think of any inducement the mere mention of which would not be ridiculously incommensurate, he proceeded: "I wouldn't do it! What you want to get married for? What do married people do, except just come home tired, and worry around and kind of scold? You better not do it, M'rice; you'll be mighty sorry."

"Everybody gets married," stated Maurice, holding his ground. "They gotta."

"I'll bet *I* don't!" Sam returned hotly. "They better catch me before they tell *me* I have to. Anyway, I bet nobody has to get married unless they want to."

"They do, too," insisted Maurice. "They *gotta!*"

"Who told you?"

"Look at what my own papa told me!" cried Maurice, heated with argument. "Didn't he tell me your papa had to marry your mamma, or else he never'd got to handle a cent of her money? Certumly, people gotta marry. Everybody. You don't know anybody over twenty years old that isn't married — except maybe teachers."

"Look at policemen!" shouted Sam triumphantly. "You don't s'pose anybody can make policemen get married, I reckon, do you?"

"Well, policemen, maybe," Maurice was forced

to admit. "Policemen and teachers don't, but everybody else gotta."

"Well, I'll be a policeman," said Sam. "*Then* I guess they won't come around tellin' me I have to get married. What you goin' to be, Penrod?"

"Chief police," said the laconic Penrod.

"What you?" Sam inquired of quiet Georgie Bassett.

"I am going to be," said Georgie, consciously, "a minister."

This announcement created a sensation so profound that it was followed by silence. Herman was the first to speak.

"You mean preachuh?" he asked incredulously. "You go' *preach?*"

"Yes," answered Georgie, looking like Saint Cecilia at the organ.

Herman was impressed. "You know all 'at preachuh talk?"

"I'm going to learn it," said Georgie simply.

"How loud kin you holler?" asked Herman doubtfully.

"He can't holler at all," Penrod interposed with scorn. "He hollers like a girl. He's the poorest hollerer in town!"

Herman shook his head. Evidently he thought Georgie's chance of being ordained very slender. Nevertheless, a final question put to the candidate by the coloured expert seemed to admit one ray of hope.

"How good kin you clim a pole?"

"He can't climb one at all," Penrod answered for Georgie. "Over at Sam's turning-pole you ought to see him try to ——"

"Preachers don't have to climb poles," Georgie said with dignity.

"*Good* ones do," declared Herman. "Bes' one ev' *I* hear, he clim up an' down same as a circus man. One n'em big 'vivals outen whens we livin' on a fahm, prechuh clim big pole right in a middle o' the church, what was to hol' roof up. He clim way high up, an' holler: 'Goin' to heavum, goin' to heavum, goin' to heavum *now*. Hallelujah, praise my Lawd!' An' he slide down little, an' holler: 'Devil's got a hol' o' my coat-tails; devil tryin' to drag me down! Sinnuhs, take wawnun! Devil got a hol' o' my coat-tails; I'm a-goin' to hell, oh Lawd!' Nex', he clim up little mo', an' yell an' holler: 'Done shuck ole devil loose; goin' straight to heavum agin! Goin' to heavum, goin' to heavum, my Lawd!' Nex', he slide down some mo' an' holler, 'Leggo my coat-tails, ole devil! Goin' to hell agin, sinnuhs! Goin' straight to hell, my Lawd!' An' he clim an he slide, an' he slide, an' he clim, an' all time holler: 'Now 'm a-goin' to heavum; now 'm a-goin' to hell! Goin' to heavum, heavum, heavum, my Lawd!' Las' he slide all a-way down, jes' a-squallin' an' a-kickin' an' a-rarin' up an' squealin', 'Goin' to hell. Goin' to hell! Ole Satum got my soul! Goin' to hell! Goin' to hell! Goin' to hell, hell, hell'!'"

Herman possessed that extraordinary facility for vivid acting which is the great native gift of his race, and he enchained his listeners. They sat fascinated and spellbound.

"Herman, tell that again!" said Penrod, breathlessly.

Herman, nothing loath, accepted the encore and repeated the Miltonic episode, expanding it somewhat, and dwelling with a fine art upon those portions of the narrative which he perceived to be most exciting to his audience. Plainly, they thrilled less to Paradise gained than to its losing, and the dreadful climax of the descent into the Pit was the greatest treat of all.

The effect was immense and instant. Penrod sprang to his feet.

"Georgie Bassett couldn't do that to save his

life," he declared. "*I*'m goin' to be a preacher! *I'd* be all right for one, wouldn't I, Herman?"

"So am I!" Sam Williams echoed loudly. "I guess I can do it if *you* can. I'd be better'n Penrod, wouldn't I, Herman?"

"I am, too!" Maurice shouted. "I got a stronger voice than anybody here, and I'd like to know what——"

The three clamoured together indistinguishably, each asserting his qualifications for the ministry according to Herman's theory, which had been accepted by these sudden converts without question.

"Listen to *me!*" Maurice bellowed, proving his claim to at least the voice by drowning the others. "Maybe I can't climb a pole so good, but who can holler louder'n this? Listen to *me-e-e!*"

"Shut up!" cried Penrod, irritated. "Go to heaven; go to hell!"

"Oo-o-oh!" exclaimed Georgie Bassett, profoundly shocked.

Sam and Maurice, awed by Penrod's daring, ceased from turmoil, staring wide-eyed.

"You cursed and swore!" said Georgie.

"I did not!" cried Penrod, hotly. "That isn't swearing."

"You said, 'Go to a big H'!" said Georgie.

"I did not! I said, 'Go to heaven,' before I said a big H. That isn't swearing, is it, Herman? It's almost what the preacher said, ain't it, Herman? It ain't swearing now, any more — not if you put 'go to heaven' with it, is it, Herman? You can say it all you want to, long as you say 'go to heaven' first, *can't* you, Herman? Anybody can say it if the preacher says it, can't they, Herman? I guess I know when I ain't swearing, don't I, Herman?"

Judge Herman ruled for the defendant, and Penrod was considered to have carried his point. With fine consistency, the conclave established that it was proper for the general public to "say it," provided "go to heaven" should in all cases precede it. This prefix was pronounced a perfect disinfectant, removing all odour of impiety or insult; and, with the exception of Georgie Bassett (who maintained that the minister's words were "going" and "gone," not "go"), all the boys proceeded to exercise their new privilege so lavishly that they tired of it.

But there was no diminution of evangelical ardour; again were heard the clamours of dispute as to which was the best qualified for the ministry, each of the claimants appealing passionately to Herman, who, pleased but confused, appeared to be incapable of arriving at a decision.

During a pause, Georgie Bassett asserted his prior rights. "Who said it first, I'd like to know?" he demanded. "I was going to be a minister from long back of to-day, I guess. And I guess I said I was going to be a minister right to-day before any of you said anything at all. *Didn't* I, Herman? *You* heard me, didn't you, Herman? That's the very thing started you talking about it, wasn't it, Herman?"

"You' right," said Herman. "You the firs' one to say it."

Penrod, Sam, and Maurice immediately lost faith in Herman. They turned from him and fell hotly upon Georgie.

"What if you did say it first?" Penrod shouted. "You couldn't *be* a minister if you were a hunderd years old!"

"I bet his mother wouldn't let him be one," said Sam. "She never lets him do anything."

"She would, too," retorted Georgie. "Ever since I was little, she ——"

"He's too sissy to be a preacher!" cried Maurice. "Listen at his squeaky voice!"

"I'm going to be a better minister," shouted Georgie, "than all three of you put together. I could do it with my left hand!"

The three laughed bitingly in chorus. They jeered, derided, scoffed, and raised an uproar which would have had its effect upon much stronger nerves than Georgie's. For a time he contained his rising choler and chanted monotonously, over and over: "*I could! I could, too! I could! I could, too!*" But their tumult wore upon him, and he decided to avail himself of the recent decision whereby a big H was rendered innocuous and unprofane. Having used the expression once, he found it comforting, and substituted it for: "I could! I could, too!"

But it relieved him only temporarily. His tormentors were unaffected by it and increased their howlings, until at last Georgie lost his head altogether. Badgered beyond bearing, his eyes shining with a wild light, he broke through the besieging trio, hurling little Maurice from his path with a frantic hand.

"I'll show you!" he cried, in this sudden frenzy. "You give me a chance, and I'll prove it right *now!*"

"That's talkin' business!" shouted Penrod. "Everybody keep still a minute. Everybody!"

He took command of the situation at once, displaying a fine capacity for organization and system. It needed only a few minutes to set order in the place of confusion and to determine, with the full concurrence of all parties, the conditions under which Georgie Bassett was to defend his claim by undergoing what may be perhaps intelligibly defined as the Herman test. Georgie declared he could do it easily. He was in a state of great excitement and in no condition to think calmly or, probably, he would not have made the attempt at all. Certainly he was overconfident.

CHAPTER XXVII

CONCLUSION OF THE QUIET AFTERNOON

IT WAS during the discussion of the details of this enterprise that Georgie's mother, a short distance down the street, received a few female callers, who came by appointment to drink a glass of iced tea with her, and to meet the Rev. Mr. Kinosling. Mr. Kinosling was proving almost formidably interesting to the women and girls of his own and other flocks. What favour of his fellow clergymen a slight preciousness of manner and pronunciation cost him was more than balanced by the visible ecstasies of ladies. They blossomed at his touch.

He had just entered Mrs. Bassett's front door, when the son of the house, followed by an intent and earnest company of four, opened the alley gate and came into the yard. The unconscious Mrs. Bassett was about to have her first, experience of a fatal coincidence. It was her first, because she was the mother of a boy so well behaved that he had become a proverb of transcendency. Fatal coincidences were plentiful in the Schofield and Williams families, and would have been familiar to Mrs. Bassett had Georgie been permitted greater intimacy with Penrod and Sam.

Mr. Kinosling sipped his iced tea and looked about him approvingly. Seven ladies leaned forward, for it was to be seen that he meant to speak.

"This cool room is a relief," he said, waving a graceful hand in a neatly limited gesture, which everybody's eyes followed, his own included. "It is a relief and a retreat. The windows open, the blinds closed — that is as it should be. It is a retreat, a fastness, a bastion against the heat's assault. For me, a quiet room — a quiet room and a book, a volume in the hand, held lightly between the fingers. A volume of poems, lines metrical and cadenced; something by a sound Victorian. We have no later poets."

"Swinburne?" suggested Miss Beam, an eager spinster. "Swinburne, Mr. Kinosling? Ah, *Swinburne!*"

"Not Swinburne," said Mr. Kinosling chastely. "No."

That concluded all the remarks about Swinburne.

Miss Beam retired in confusion behind another lady; and somehow there became diffused an impression that Miss Beam was erotic.

"I do not observe your manly little son," Mr. Kinosling addressed his hostess.

"He's out playing in the yard," Mrs. Bassett returned. "I heard his voice just now, I think."

"Everywhere I hear wonderful report of him," said Mr. Kinosling. "I may say that I understand boys, and I feel that he is a rare, a fine, a pure, a lofty spirit. I say spirit, for spirit is the word I hear spoken of him."

A chorus of enthusiastic approbation affirmed the accuracy of this proclamation, and Mrs. Bassett flushed with pleasure. Georgie's spiritual perfection was demonstrated by instances of it, related by the visitors; his piety was cited, and wonderful things he had said were quoted.

"Not all boys are pure, of fine spirit, of high mind," said Mr. Kinosling, and continued with true feeling: "You have a neighbour, dear Mrs. Bassett, whose household I indeed really feel it quite impossible to visit until such time when better, firmer, stronger handed, more determined discipline shall prevail. I find Mr. and Mrs. Schofield and their daughter charming, but ——"

Three or four ladies said "Oh!" and spoke a name simultaneously. It was as if they had said, "Oh, the bubonic plague!"

"Oh! Penrod Schofield!"

"Georgie does not play with him," said Mrs. Bassett quickly — "that is, he avoids him as much as he can without hurting Penrod's feelings. Georgie is very sensitive to giving pain. I suppose a mother should not tell these things, and I know people who talk about their own children are dreadful bores, but it was only last Thursday night that Georgie looked up in my face so sweetly, after he had said his prayers and his little cheeks flushed, as he said: "Mamma, I think it would be right for me to go more with Penrod. I think it would make him a better boy."

A sibilance went about the room. "Sweet! How sweet! The sweet little soul! Ah, *sweet!*"

"And that very afternoon," continued Mrs. Bassett, "he had come home in a dreadful state. Penrod had thrown tar all over him."

"Your son has a forgiving spirit!" said Mr. Kinosling with vehemence. "A too forgiving spirit, perhaps." He set down his glass. "No more, I thank you. No more cake, I thank you. Was it not Cardinal Newman who said ——"

He was interrupted by the sounds of an altercation just outside the closed blinds of the window nearest him.

"Let him pick his tree!" It was the voice of Samuel Williams. "Didn't we come over here to give him one of his own trees? Give him a fair show, can't you?"

"The little lads!" Mr. Kinosling smiled. "They have their games, their outdoor sports, their pastimes. The young muscles are toughening. The sun will not harm them. They grow; they expand; they learn. They learn fair play, honour, courtesy, from one another, as pebbles grow round in the brook. They learn more from themselves than from us. They take shape, form, outline. Let them."

"Mr. Kinosling!" Another spinster — undeterred by what had happened to Miss Beam — leaned far forward, her face shining and ardent. "Mr. Kinosling, there's a question I *do* wish to ask you."

"My dear Miss Cosslit," Mr. Kinosling responded, again waving his hand and watching it, "I am entirely at your disposal."

"*Was* Joan of Arc," she asked fervently "inspired by spirits?"

He smiled indulgently. "Yes — and no," he said. "One must give both answers. One must give the answer, yes; one must give the answer, no."

"Oh, *thank* you!" said Miss Cosslit, blushing. "She's one of my great enthusiasms, you know."

"And I have a question, too," urged Mrs. Lora Rewbush, after a moment's hasty concentration. "I've never been able to settle it for myself, but *now* ——"

"Yes?" said Mr. Kinosling encouragingly.

"Is — ah — is — oh, yes: Is Sanskrit a more difficult language than Spanish, Mr. Kinosling?"

"It depends upon the student," replied the oracle, smiling. "One must not look for linguists everywhere. In my own especial case — if one may cite one's self as an example — I found no great, no insurmountable difficulty in mastering, in conquering either."

"And may *I* ask one?" ventured Mrs. Bassett. "Do you think it is right to wear egrets?"

"There are marks of quality, of caste, of social distinction," Mr. Kinosling began, "which must be permitted, allowed, though perhaps regulated. Social distinction, one observes, almost invariably implies spiritual distinction as well. Distinction of circumstances is accompanied by mental distinction. Distinction is hereditary; it descends from father to son, and if there is one thing more true than 'Like father, like son,' it is —" he bowed gallantly to Mrs. Bassett — "it is, 'Like mother, like son.' What these good ladies have said this afternoon of *your* ——"

This was the fatal instant. There smote upon all ears the voice of Georgie, painfully shrill and penetrating — fraught with protest and protracted strain. His plain words consisted of the newly sanctioned and disinfected curse with a big H.

With an ejaculation of horror, Mrs. Bassett sprang to the window and threw open the blinds.

Georgie's back was disclosed to the view of the tea-party. He was endeavouring to ascend a maple tree about twelve feet from the window. Embracing the trunk with arms and legs, he had managed to squirm to a point just above the heads of Penrod and Herman, who stood close by, watching him earnestly — Penrod being obviously in charge of the performance. Across the yard were Sam Williams and Maurice Levy, acting as a jury on the question of voice-power, and it was to a complaint of theirs that Georgie had just replied.

"That's right, Georgie," said Penrod encouragingly. "They can, too, hear you. Let her go!"

"Going to heaven!" shrieked Georgie, squirming up another inch. "Going to heaven, heaven, heaven!"

His mother's frenzied attempts to attract his attention failed utterly. Georgie was using the full power of his lungs, deafening his own ears to all other sounds. Mrs. Bassett called in vain; while the tea-party stood petrified in a cluster about the window.

"Going to heaven!" Georgie bellowed. "Going to heaven! Going to heaven, my Lord! Going to heaven, heaven, heaven!"

He tried to climb higher, but began to slip downward, his exertions causing damage to his apparel. A button flew into the air, and his knickerbockers and his waistband severed relations.

"Devil's got my coat-tails, sinners! Old devil's

got my coat-tails!" he announced appropriately. Then he began to slide. He relaxed his clasp of the tree and slid to the ground.

"Going to hell!" shrieked Georgie, reaching a high pitch of enthusiasm in this great climax. "Going to hell! Going to hell! I'm gone to hell, hell, hell!"

With a loud scream, Mrs. Bassett threw herself out of the window, alighting by some miracle upon her feet with ankles unsprained.

Mr. Kinosling, feeling that his presence as spiritual adviser was demanded in the yard, followed with greater dignity through the front door. At the corner of the house a small departing figure collided with him violently. It was Penrod, tactfully withdrawing from what promised to be a family scene of unusual painfulness.

Mr. Kinosling seized him by the shoulders and, giving way to emotion, shook him viciously.

"You horrible boy!" exclaimed Mr. Kinosling. "You ruffianly creature! Do you know what's going to happen to you when you grow up? Do you realize what you're going to *be!*"

With flashing eyes, the indignant boy made known his unshaken purpose. He shouted the reply:

"A minister!"

CHAPTER XXVIII

TWELVE

THIS busy globe which spawns us is as incapable of flattery and as intent upon its own affair, whatever that is, as a gyroscope; it keeps steadily whirling along its lawful track, and, thus far seeming to hold a right of way, spins doggedly on, with no perceptible diminution of speed to mark the most gigantic human events — it did not pause to pant and recuperate even when what seemed to Penrod its principal purpose was accomplished, and an enormous shadow, vanishing westward over its surface, marked the dawn of his twelfth birthday.

To be twelve is an attainment worth the struggle.

A boy, just twelve, is like a Frenchman just elected to the Academy.

Distinction and honour wait upon him. Younger boys show deference to a person of twelve: his experience is guaranteed, his judgment, therefore, mellow; consequently, his influence is profound. Eleven is not quite satisfactory: it is only an approach. Eleven has the disadvantage of six, of nineteen, of forty-four, and of sixty-nine. But, like twelve, seven is an honourable age, and the ambition to attain it is laudable. People look forward to being seven. Similarly, twenty is worthy, and so, arbitrarily, is twenty-one; forty-five has great solidity; seventy is most commendable and each year thereafter an increasing honour. Thirteen is embarrassed by the beginnings of a new colthood; the child becomes a youth. But twelve is the very top of boyhood.

Dressing, that morning, Penrod felt that the world was changed from the world of yesterday. For one thing, he seemed to own more of it; this day was *his* day. And it was a day worth owning; the midsummer sunshine, pouring gold through his window, came from a cool sky, and a breeze moved pleasantly in his hair as he leaned from the sill to watch the tribe of chattering blackbirds take wing, following their leader from the trees in the yard to the day's work in the open country. The blackbirds were his, as the sunshine and the breeze were his, for they all belonged to the day which was his birthday and therefore most surely his. Pride suffused him: he was Twelve!

His father and his mother and Margaret seemed to understand the difference between to-day and yesterday. They were at the table when he descended, and they gave him a greeting which of itself marked the milestone. Habitually, his entrance into a room where his elders sat brought a cloud of apprehension: they were prone to look up in pathetic expectancy, as if their thought was, "What new awfulness is he going to start *now?*" But this morning they laughed; his mother rose and kissed him twelve times, so did Margaret; and his father shouted, "Well, well! How's the *man?*"

Then his mother gave him a Bible and "The Vicar of Wakefield"; Margaret gave him a pair of silver-mounted hair brushes; and his father gave him a "Pocket Atlas" and a small compass.

"And now, Penrod," said his mother, after breakfast, "I'm going to take you out in the country to pay your birthday respects to Aunt Sarah Crim."

Aunt Sarah Crim, Penrod's great-aunt, was his oldest living relative. She was ninety, and when Mrs. Schofield and Penrod alighted from a carriage at her gate they found her digging with a spade in the garden.

"I'm glad you brought him," she said, desisting from labour. "Jinny's baking a cake I'm going to send for his birthday party. Bring him in the house. I've got something for him."

She led the way to her "sitting-room," which had a pleasant smell, unlike any other smell, and, opening the drawer of a shining old what-not, took therefrom a boy's "sling-shot," made of a forked stick, two strips of rubber and a bit of leather.

"This isn't for you," she said, placing it in Penrod's eager hand. "No. It would break all to pieces the first time you tried to shoot it, because it is thirty-five years old. I want to send it back to your father. I think it's time. You give it to him from me, and tell him I say I believe I can trust him with it now. I took it away from him thirty-five years ago, one day after he'd killed my best hen with it, accidentally, and broken a glass pitcher on

the back porch with it — accidentally. He doesn't
look like a person who's ever done things of that
sort, and I suppose he's forgotten it so well that he
believes he never *did*, but if you give it to him from
me I think he'll remember. You look like him,
Penrod. He was anything but a handsome boy."

After this final bit of reminiscence — probably
designed to be repeated to Mr. Schofield — she disappeared in the direction of the kitchen, and returned with a pitcher of lemonade and a blue china
dish sweetly freighted with flat ginger cookies of a
composition that was her own secret. Then, having set this collation before her guests, she presented
Penrod with a superb, intricate, and very modern
machine of destructive capacities almost limitless.
She called it a pocket-knife.

"I suppose you'll do something horrible with
it," she said, composedly. "I hear you do that
with everything, anyhow, so you might as well do
it with this, and have more fun out of it. They tell
me you're the Worst Boy in Town."

"Oh, Aunt Sarah!" Mrs. Schofield lifted a protesting hand.

"Nonsense!" said Mrs. Crim.

"But, on his birthday!"

"That's the time to say it. Penrod, aren't you the Worst Boy in Town?"

Penrod, gazing fondly upon his knife and eating cookies rapidly, answered as a matter of course, and absently, "Yes'm."

"Certainly!" said Mrs. Crim. "Once you accept a thing about yourself as established and settled, it's all right. Nobody minds. Boys are just like people, really."

"No, no!" Mrs. Schofield cried, involuntarily.

"Yes, they are," returned Aunt Sarah. "Only they're not quite so awful, because they haven't learned to cover themselves all over with little pretences. When Penrod grows up he'll be just the same as he is now, except that whenever he does what he wants to do he'll tell himself and other people a little story about it to make his reason for doing it seem nice and pretty and noble."

"No, I won't!" said Penrod suddenly.

"There's one cookie left," observed Aunt Sarah. "Are you going to eat it?"

"Well," said her great-nephew, thoughtfully, "I guess I better."

"Why?" asked the old lady. "Why do you guess you'd 'better'?"

"Well," said Penrod, with a full mouth, "it might get all dried up if nobody took it, and get thrown out and wasted."

"You're beginning finely," Mrs. Crim remarked. "A year ago you'd have taken the cookie without the same sense of thrift."

"Ma'am?"

"Nothing. I see that you're twelve years old, that's all. There are more cookies, Penrod." She went away, returning with a fresh supply and the observation, "Of course, you'll be sick before the day's over; you might as well get a good start."

Mrs. Schofield looked thoughtful. "Aunt Sarah," she ventured, "don't you really think we improve as we get older?"

"Meaning," said the old lady, "that Penrod hasn't much chance to escape the penitentiary if he doesn't? Well, we do learn to restrain ourselves in some things; and there are people who really want some one else to take the last cookie, though they aren't very common. But it's all right, the world seems to be getting on." She gazed whimsically upon her great-nephew and added, "Of course, when you watch a boy and think about him, it doesn't seem to be getting on very fast."

Penrod moved uneasily in his chair; he was conscious that he was her topic but unable to make out whether or not her observations were complimentary; he inclined to think they were not. Mrs. Crim settled the question for him.

"I suppose Penrod is regarded as the neighbourhood curse?"

"Oh, no," cried Mrs. Schofield. "He ——"

"I dare say the neighbours are right," continued the old lady placidly. "He's had to repeat the history of the race and go through all the stages from the primordial to barbarism. You don't expect boys to be civilized, do you?"

"Well, I ——"

"You might as well expect eggs to crow. No; you've got to take boys as they are, and learn to know them as they are."

"Naturally, Aunt Sarah," said Mrs. Schofield, "I *know* Penrod."

Aunt Sarah laughed heartily. "Do you think his father knows him, too?"

"Of course, men are different," Mrs. Schofield returned, apologetically. "But a mother knows ——"

"Penrod," said Aunt Sarah, solemnly, "does your father understand you?"

"Ma'am?"

"About as much as he'd understand Sitting Bull!" she laughed. "And I'll tell you what your mother thinks you are, Penrod. Her real belief is that you're a novice in a convent."

"Ma'am?"

"Aunt Sarah!"

"I know she thinks that, because whenever you don't behave like a novice she's disappointed in you. And your father really believes that you're a decorous, well-trained young business man, and whenever you don't live up to that standard you get on his nerves and he thinks you need a walloping. I'm sure a day very seldom passes without their both saying they don't know what on earth to do with you. Does whipping do you any good, Penrod?"

"Ma'am?"

"Go on and finish the lemonade; there's about a glassful left. Oh, take it, take it; and don't say why! Of *course* you're a little pig."

Penrod laughed gratefully, his eyes fixed upon her over the rim of his uptilted glass.

"Fill yourself up uncomfortably," said the old lady. "You're twelve years old, and you ought to be happy — if you aren't anything else. It's taken over nineteen hundred years of Christianity and some hundreds of thousands of years of other things to produce you, and there you sit!"

"Ma'am?"

"It'll be your turn to struggle and muss things up for the betterment of posterity, soon enough," said Aunt Sarah Crim. "Drink your lemonade!"

CHAPTER XXIX

FANCHON

"AUNT SARAH'S a funny old lady," Penrod observed, on the way back to the town. "What's she want me to give papa this old sling for? Last thing she said was to be sure not to forget to give it to him. *He* don't want it; and she said, herself, it ain't any good. She's older than you or papa, isn't she?"

"About fifty years older," answered Mrs. Scho-field, turning upon him a stare of perplexity. "Don't cut into the leather with your new knife, dear; the liv-ery man might ask us to pay if —— No, I wouldn't scrape the paint off, either — nor whittle your shoe with it. *Couldn't* you put it up until we get home?"

"We goin' straight home?"

"No. We're going to stop at Mrs. Gelbraith's and ask a strange little girl to come to your party, this afternoon."

"Who?"

"Her name is Fanchon. She's Mrs. Gelbraith's little niece."

"What makes her so queer?"

"I didn't say she's queer."

"You said ——"

"No; I mean that she is a stranger. She lives in New York and has come to visit here."

"What's she live in New York for?"

"Because her parents live there. You must be very nice to her, Penrod; she has been very carefully brought up. Besides, she doesn't know the children here, and you must help to keep her from feeling lonely at your party."

"Yes'm."

When they reached Mrs. Gelbraith's, Penrod sat patiently humped upon a gilt chair during the lengthy exchange of greetings between his mother and Mrs. Gelbraith. That is one of the things a boy must learn to bear: when his mother meets a compeer there is always a long and dreary wait for him, while the two appear to be using strange symbols of speech, talking for the greater part, it seems to him, simultaneously, and employing a wholly incomprehensible system of emphasis at other times not in vogue. Penrod twisted his legs, his cap and his nose.

"Here she is!" Mrs. Gelbraith cried, unexpectedly, and a dark-haired, demure person entered the room wearing a look of gracious social expectancy. In years she was eleven, in manner about sixty-five, and evidently had lived much at court. She performed a curtsey in acknowledgment of Mrs. Schofield's greeting, and bestowed her hand upon Penrod, who had entertained no hope of such an honour, showed his surprise that it should come to him, and was plainly unable to decide what to do about it.

"Fanchon, dear," said Mrs. Gelbraith, "take Penrod out in the yard for a while, and play."

"Let go the little girl's hand, Penrod," Mrs Schofield laughed, as the children turned toward the door.

Penrod hastily dropped the small hand, and exclaiming, with simply honesty, "Why, *I* don't want it!" followed Fanchon out into the sunshiny yard, where they came to a halt and surveyed each other.

Penrod stared awkwardly at Fanchon, no other occupation suggesting itself to him, while Fanchon, with the utmost coolness, made a very thorough visual examination of Penrod, favouring him with an estimating scrutiny which lasted until he literally wiggled. Finally, she spoke.

"Where do you buy your ties?" she asked.

"What?"

"Where do you buy your neckties? Papa gets his at Skoone's. You ought to get yours there. I'm sure the one you're wearing isn't from Skoone's."

"Skoone's?" Penrod repeated. "Skoone's?"

"On Fifth Avenue," said Fanchon. "It's a very smart shop, the men say."

"Men?" echoed Penrod, in a hazy whisper. "Men?"

"Where do your people go in summer?" inquired the lady. "*We* go to Long Shore, but so many middle-class people have begun coming there, mamma thinks of leaving. The middle classes are simply awful, don't you think?"

"What?"

"They're so boorjaw. You speak French, of course?"

"Me?"

"We ran over to Paris last year. It's lovely, don't you think? Don't you *love* the Rue de la Paix?"

Penrod wandered in a labyrinth. This girl seemed to be talking, but her words were dumfounding, and of course there was no way for him to know that he was really listening to her mother. It was his first meeting with one of those grown-up little girls, wonderful product of the winter apartment and summer hotel; and Fanchon, an only child, was a star of the brand. He began to feel resentful.

"I suppose," she went on, "I'll find everything here fearfully Western. Some nice people called yesterday, though. Do you know the Magsworth Bittses? Auntie says they're charming. Will Roddy be at your party?"

"I guess he will," returned Penrod, finding this intelligible. "The mutt!"

"Really!" Fanchon exclaimed airily. "Aren't you great pals with him?"

"What's 'pals'?"

"Good heavens! Don't you know what it means to say you're 'great pals' with any one? You *are* an odd child!"

It was too much.

"Oh, Bugs!" said Penrod.

This bit of ruffianism had a curious effect. Fanchon looked upon him with sudden favour.

"I like you, Penrod!" she said, in an odd way, and, whatever else there may have been in her manner, there certainly was no shyness.

"Oh, Bugs!" This repetition may have lacked gallantry, but it was uttered in no very decided tone. Penrod was shaken.

"Yes, I do!" She stepped closer to him, smiling. "Your hair is ever so pretty."

Sailors' parrots swear like mariners, they say; and gay mothers ought to realize that all children are imitative, for, as the precocious Fanchon leaned toward Penrod, the manner in which she looked into his eyes might have made a thoughtful observer wonder where she had learned her pretty ways.

Penrod was even more confused than he had been by her previous mysteries: but his confusion was of a distinctly pleasant and alluring nature: he wanted more of it. Looking intentionally into another person's eyes is an act unknown to childhood; and Penrod's discovery that it could be done was sensational. He had never thought of looking into the eyes of Marjorie Jones.

Despite all anguish, contumely, tar, and Maurice

Levy, he still secretly thought of Marjorie, with pathetic constancy, as his "beau" — though that is not how he would have spelled it. Marjorie was beautiful; her curls were long and the colour of amber; her nose was straight and her freckles were honest; she was much prettier than this accomplished visitor. But beauty is not all.

"I do!" breathed Fanchon, softly.

She seemed to him a fairy creature from some rosier world than this. So humble is the human heart, it glorifies and makes glamorous almost any poor thing that says to it: "I like you!"

Penrod was enslaved. He swallowed, coughed, scratched the back of his neck, and said, disjointedly:

"Well — I don't care — if you want to. I just as soon."

"We'll dance together," said Fanchon, "at your party."

"I guess so. I just as soon."

"Don't you want to, Penrod?"

"Well, I'm willing to."

"No. Say you *want* to!"

"Well ——"

He used his toe as a gimlet, boring into the ground, his wide open eyes staring with intense vacancy at

a button on his sleeve.   His mother appeared upon
the porch in departure, calling farewells over her
shoulder to Mrs. Gelbraith, who stood in the doorway.

"Say it!" whispered Fanchon.

"Well, I just as *soon*."

She seemed satisfied.

CHAPTER XXX

THE BIRTHDAY PARTY

A DANCING floor had been laid upon a platform in the yard, when Mrs. Schofield and
her son arrived at their own abode; and a
white and scarlet striped canopy was in process of
erection overhead, to shelter the dancers from the
sun. Workmen were busy everywhere under the
direction of Margaret, and the smitten heart of
Penrod began to beat rapidly. All this was for
him; he was Twelve!

After lunch, he underwent an elaborate toilette
and murmured not. For the first time in his life

he knew the wish to be sand-papered, waxed, and polished to the highest possible degree. And when the operation was over, he stood before the mirror in new bloom, feeling encouraged to hope that his resemblance to his father was not so strong as Aunt Sarah seemed to think.

The white gloves upon his hands had a pleasant smell, he found; and, as he came down the stairs, he had great content in the twinkling of his new dancing slippers. He stepped twice on each step, the better to enjoy their effect and at the same time he deeply inhaled the odour of the gloves. In spite of everything, Penrod had his social capacities. Already it is to be perceived that there were in him the makings of a cotillon leader.

Then came from the yard a sound of tuning instruments, squeak of fiddle, croon of 'cello, a falling triangle ringing and tinkling to the floor; and he turned pale.

Chosen guests began to arrive, while Penrod, suffering from stage-fright and perspiration, stood beside his mother, in the "drawing-room," to receive them. He greeted unfamiliar acquaintances and intimate fellow-criminals with the same frigidity, murmuring: "'M glad to see y'," to all alike.

largely increasing the embarrassment which always prevails at the beginning of children's festivities. His unnatural pomp and circumstance had so thoroughly upset him, in truth, that Marjorie Jones received a distinct shock, now to be related. Doctor Thrope, the kind old clergyman who had baptized Penrod, came in for a moment to congratulate the boy, and had just moved away when it was Marjorie's turn, in the line of children, to speak to Penrod. She gave him what she considered a forgiving look, and, because of the occasion, addressed him in a perfectly courteous manner.

"I wish you many happy returns of the day, Penrod."

"Thank you, sir!" he returned, following Dr. Thrope with a glassy stare in which there was absolutely no recognition of Marjorie. Then he greeted Maurice Levy, who was next to Marjorie: "'M glad to see y'!"

Dumfounded, Marjorie turned aside, and stood near, observing Penrod with gravity. It was the first great surprise of her life. Customarily, she had seemed to place his character somewhere between that of the professional rioter and that of the orang-outang; nevertheless, her manner at times just hinted a consciousness that this Caliban was her property. Wherefore, she stared at him incredulously as his head bobbed up and down, in the dancing-school bow, greeting his guests. Then she heard an adult voice, near her, exclaim:

"What an exquisite child!"

Marjorie glanced up — a little consciously, though she was used to it — naturally curious to ascertain who was speaking of her. It was Sam Williams' mother addressing Mrs. Bassett, both being present to help Mrs. Schofield make the festivities festive.

"Exquisite!"

Here was a second heavy surprise for Marjorie: they were not looking at her. They were looking with beaming approval at a girl she had never seen; a dark and modish stranger of singularly composed and yet modest aspect. Her downcast eyes, becoming in one thus entering a crowded room, were all that produced the effect of modesty, counteracting something about her which might have seemed too assured. She was very slender, very dainty, and her apparel was disheartening to the other girls; it was of a knowing picturesqueness wholly unfamiliar to them. There was a delicate trace of powder upon the lobe of Fanchon's left ear, and the outlines of her eyelids, if very closely scrutinized, would have revealed successful experimentation with a burnt match.

Marjorie's lovely eyes dilated: she learned the meaning of hatred at first sight. Observing the stranger with instinctive suspicion, all at once she seemed, to herself, awkward. Poor Marjorie underwent that experience which hearty, healthy, little girls and big girls undergo at one time or another — from heels to head she felt herself, somehow, too *thick*.

Fanchon leaned close to Penrod and whispered in his ear:

"Don't you forget!"

Penrod blushed.

Marjorie saw the blush. Her lovely eyes opened even wider, and in them there began to grow a light. It was the light of indignation; — at least, people whose eyes glow with that light always call it indignation.

Roderick Magsworth Bitts, Junior, approached Fanchon, when she had made her courtesy to Mrs. Schofield. Fanchon whispered in Roderick's ear also.

"Your hair *is* pretty, Roddy! Don't forget what you said yesterday!"

Roderick likewise blushed.

Maurice Levy, captivated by the newcomer's appearance, pressed close to Roderick.

"Give us an intaduction, Roddy?"

Roddy being either reluctant or unable to perform the rite, Fanchon took matters into her own hands, and was presently favourably impressed with Maurice, receiving the information that his tie had been brought to him by his papa from Skoone's, whereupon she privately informed him that she liked wavy hair, and arranged to dance with him. Fanchon also thought sandy hair attractive, Sam Williams discovered, a few minutes later; and so catholic was her taste that a ring of boys quite encircled her before the musicians in the yard struck up their thrilling march, and Mrs. Schofield brought Penrod to escort the lady from out-of-town to the dancing pavilion.

Headed by this pair, the children sought partners and paraded solemnly out of the front door and round a corner of the house. There they found the gay marquee; the small orchestra seated on the lawn at one side of it, and a punch bowl of lemonade inviting attention, under a tree. Decorously the small couples stepped upon the platform, one after another, and began to dance.

"It's not much like a children's party in our day," Mrs. Williams said to Penrod's mother. "We'd have been playing 'Quaker-meeting,' 'Clap-in, Clap-out,' or 'Going to Jerusalem,' I suppose."

"Yes, or 'Post-office' and 'Drop-the-handker-chief,'" said Mrs. Schofield. 'Things change so quickly. Imagine asking little Fanchon Gelbraith to play 'London Bridge'! Penrod seems to be having a difficult time with her, poor boy; he wasn't a shining light in the dancing class."

However, Penrod's difficulty was not precisely of the kind his mother supposed. Fanchon was showing him a new step, which she taught her next partner in turn, continuing instructions during the dancing. The children crowded the floor, and in the kaleidoscopic jumble of bobbing heads and inter-mingling figures her extremely different style of motion was unobserved by the older people, who looked on, nodding time benevolently.

Fanchon fascinated girls as well as boys. Many of the former eagerly sought her acquaintance and thronged about her between the dances, when, ac-cepting the deference due a cosmopolitan and an oracle of the mode, she gave demonstrations of the new step to succeeding groups, professing astonishment to find it unknown: it had been "all the go," she explained, at the Long Shore Casino for fully two seasons. She pronounced "slow" a "Fancy Dance" executed during an intermission by Baby Rennsdale and Georgie Bassett, giving it as her opinion that Miss Rennsdale and Mr. Bassett were "dead ones"; and she expressed surprise that the punch bowl contained lemonade and not champagne.

The dancing continued, the new step gaining instantly in popularity, fresh couples adventuring with every number. The word "step" is somewhat misleading, nothing done with the feet being vital to the evolutions introduced by Fanchon. Fanchon's dance came from the Orient by a roundabout way; pausing in Spain, taking on a Gallic frankness in gallantry at the Bal Bullier in Paris, combining with a relative from the South Seas encountered in San Francisco, flavouring itself with a carefree negroid abandon in New Orleans, and, accumulating, too, something inexpressible from Mexico and South America, it kept, throughout its travels, to the underworld, or to circles where nature is extremely frank and rank, until at last it reached the dives of New York, when it immediately broke out in what is called civilized society. Thereafter it spread, in variously modified forms — some of them disinfected — to watering-places, and thence, carried by hundreds of older male and female Fanchons, over the country, being eagerly adopted everywhere and made wholly pure and respectable by the supreme moral axiom that anything is all right if enough people do it. Everybody was doing it.

Not quite everybody. It was perhaps some test of this dance that earth could furnish no more grotesque sight than that of children doing it.

Earth, assisted by Fanchon, was furnishing this sight at Penrod's party. By the time ice-cream and cake arrived, about half the guests had either been initiated into the mysteries by Fanchon or were learning by imitation, and the education of the other half was resumed with the dancing, when the attendant ladies, unconscious of what was happening, withdrew into the house for tea.

"That orchestra's a dead one," Fanchon remarked to Penrod. "We ought to liven them up a little!"

She approached the musicians.

"Don't you know," she asked the leader, "the Slingo Sligo Slide?"

The leader giggled, nodded, rapped with his bow upon his violin; and Penrod, following Fanchon back upon the dancing floor, blindly brushed with his elbow a solitary little figure standing aloof on the lawn at the edge of the platform.

It was Marjorie.

In no mood to approve of anything introduced by Fanchon, she had scornfully refused, from the first, to dance the new "step," and, because of its bonfire popularity, found herself neglected in a society where she had reigned as beauty and belle. Faithless Penrod, dazed by the sweeping Fanchon, had utterly forgotten the amber curls; he had not once asked Marjorie to dance. All afternoon the light of indignation had been growing brighter in her eyes, though Maurice Levy's defection to the lady from New York had not fanned this flame. From the moment Fanchon had whispered familiarly in Penrod's ear, and Penrod had blushed, Marjorie had been occupied exclusively with resentment against that guilty pair. It seemed to her that Penrod had no right to allow a strange girl to whisper in his ear; that his blushing, when the strange girl did it, was atrocious; and that the strange girl, herself, ought to be arrested.

Forgotten by the merrymakers, Marjorie stood alone upon the lawn, clenching her small fists, watching the new dance at its high tide, and hating it with a hatred that made every inch of her tremble. And, perhaps because jealousy is a great awakener of the virtues, she had a perception of something in it worse than lack of dignity — something vaguely but outrageously reprehensible. Finally, when Penrod brushed by her, touched her with his elbow, and did not even see her, Marjorie's state of mind (not unmingled with emotion!) became dangerous. In fact, a trained nurse, chancing to observe her at this juncture, would probably have advised that she be taken home and put to bed. Marjorie was on the verge of hysterics.

She saw Fanchon and Penrod assume the double embrace required by the dance; the "Slingo Sligo Slide" burst from the orchestra like the lunatic shriek of a gin-maddened nigger; and all the little couples began to bob and dip and sway.

Marjorie made a scene. She sprang upon the platform and stamped her foot.

"Penrod Schofield!" she shouted. "You BE-HAVE yourself!"

The remarkable girl took Penrod by the ear. By his ear she swung him away from Fanchon and faced him toward the lawn.

By his ear she swung him away from Fanchon and faced him toward the lawn

"You march straight out of here!" she commanded.

Penrod marched.

He was stunned; obeyed automatically, without question, and had very little realization of what was happening to him. Altogether, and without reason, he was in precisely the condition of an elderly spouse detected in flagrant misbehaviour. Marjorie, similarly, was in precisely the condition of the party who detects such misbehaviour. It may be added that she had acted with a promptness, a decision and a disregard of social consequences all to be commended to the attention of ladies in like predicament.

"You ought to be ashamed of yourself!" she raged, when they reached the lawn. "Aren't you ashamed of yourself?"

"What for?" he inquired, helplessly.

"You be quiet!"

"But what'd *I* do, Marjorie? *I* haven't done anything to you," he pleaded. "I haven't even seen you, all aftern ——"

"You be quiet!" she cried, tears filling her eyes. "Keep still! You ugly boy! Shut *up!*"

She slapped him.

He should have understood from this how much

she cared for him. But he rubbed his cheek and declared ruefully:

"I'll never speak to you again!"

"You will, too!" she sobbed, passionately.

"I will not!"

He turned to leave her, but paused.

His mother, his sister Margaret, and their grown-up friends had finished their tea and were approaching from the house. Other parents and guardians were with them, coming for their children; and there were carriages and automobiles waiting in the street. But the "Slingo Slide" went on, regardless.

The group of grown-up people hesitated and came to a halt, gazing at the pavilion.

"What are they doing?" gasped Mrs. Williams, blushing deeply. "What is it?   What *is* it?"

"*What is it?*" Mrs. Gelbraith echoed in a frightened whisper. "*What* ——"

"They're Tangoing!" cried Margaret Schofield. "Or Bunny Hugging or Grizzly Bearing, or ——"

"They're only Turkey Trotting," said Robert Williams.

With fearful outcries the mothers, aunts, and sisters rushed upon the pavilion.

"Of course it was dreadful," said Mrs. Schofield, an hour later, rendering her lord an account of the day, "but it was every bit the fault of that one extraordinary child. And of all the quiet, demure little things — that is, I mean, when she first came. We all spoke of how exquisite she seemed — so well trained, so finished! Eleven years old! I never saw anything like her in my life!"

"I suppose it's the New Child," her husband grunted.

"And to think of her saying there ought to have been champagne in the lemonade!"

"Probably she'd forgotten to bring her pocket flask," he suggested musingly.

"But aren't you proud of Penrod?" cried Penrod's mother. "It was just as I told you: he was standing clear outside the pavilion ——"

"I never thought to see the day! And Penrod was the only boy not doing it, the only one to refuse? *All* the others were ——"

"Every one!" she returned triumphantly. "Even Georgie Bassett!"

"Well," said Mr. Schofield, patting her on the shoulder, "I guess we can hold up our heads at last."

CHAPTER XXXI

OVER THE FENCE

PENROD was out in the yard, staring at the empty marquee. The sun was on the horizon line, so far behind the back fence, and a western window of the house blazed in gold unbearable to the eye: his day was nearly over. He sighed, and took from the inside pocket of his new jacket the "sling-shot" aunt Sarah Crim had given him that morning.

He snapped the rubbers absently. They held fast; and his next impulse was entirely irresistible. He found a shapely stone, fitted it to the leather, and drew back the ancient catapult for a shot. A sparrow hopped upon a branch between him and the house, and he aimed at the sparrow, but the reflection from the dazzling window struck in his eyes as he loosed the leather.

He missed the sparrow, but not the window. There was a loud crash, and to his horror he caught a glimpse of his father, stricken in mid-shaving, ducking a shower of broken glass, glittering razor flourishing wildly. Words crashed with the glass, stentorian words, fragmentary but collossal.

Penrod stood petrified, a broken sling in his hand. He could hear his parent's booming descent of the back stairs, instant and furious; and then, red-hot above white lather, Mr. Schofield burst out of the kitchen door and hurtled forth upon his son.

"What do you mean?" he demanded, shaking Penrod by the shoulder. "Ten minutes ago, for the very first time in our lives, your mother and I were saying we were proud of you, and here you go and throw a rock at me through the window when I'm shaving for dinner!"

"I didn't!" Penrod quavered. "I was shooting at a sparrow, and the sun got in my eyes, and the sling broke ——"

"What sling?"

"This'n."

"Where'd you get that devilish thing? Don't you know I've forbidden you a thousand times ——"

"It ain't mine," said Penrod. "It's yours."

"What?"

"Yes, sir," said the boy meekly. "Aunt Sarah Crim gave it to me this morning and told me to give it back to you. She said she took it away from you thirty-five years ago. You killed her hen, she said. She told me some more to tell you, but I've forgotten."

"Oh!" said Mr. Schofield.

He took the broken sling in his hand, looked at it long and thoughtfully — and he looked longer, and quite as thoughtfully, at Penrod. Then he turned away, and walked toward the house.

"I'm sorry, papa," said Penrod.

Mr. Schofield coughed, and, as he reached the door, called back, but without turning his head.

"Never mind, little boy. A broken window isn't much harm."

When he had gone in, Penrod wandered down the yard to the back fence, climbed upon it, and sat in reverie there.

A slight figure appeared, likewise upon a fence, beyond two neighbouring yards.

"Yay, Penrod!" called comrade Sam Williams.

"Yay!" returned Penrod, mechanically.

"I caught Billy Blue Hill!" shouted Sam, describing retribution in a manner perfect'y clear to his friend. "You were mighty lucky to get out of it."

"I know that!"

"You wouldn't of, if it hadn't been for Marjorie."

"Well, don't I know that?" Penrod shouted, with heat.

"Well, so long!" called Sam, dropping from his fence; and the friendly voice came then, more faintly, "Many happy returns of the day, Penrod!"

And now, a plaintive little whine sounded from below Penrod's feet, and, looking down, he saw that Duke, his wistful, old, scraggly dog sat in the grass, gazing seekingly up at him.

The last shaft of sunshine of that day fell graciously and like a blessing upon the boy sitting on the fence. Years afterward, a quiet sunset would recall to him sometimes the gentle evening of his twelfth birthday, and bring him the picture of his boy self, sitting in rosy light upon the fence, gazing pensively down upon his wistful, scraggly, little old dog, Duke.

But something else, surpassing, he would remember of that hour, for, in the side street, close by, a pink skirt flickered from behind a shade tree to the shelter of the fence, there was a gleam of amber curls, and Penrod started, as something like a tiny white wing fluttered by his head, and there came to his ears the sound of a light laugh and of light footsteps departing, the laughter tremulous, the footsteps fleet.

In the grass, between Duke's forepaws, there lay a white note, folded in the shape of a cocked hat, and the sun sent forth a final amazing glory as Penrod opened it and read:

"Your my Bow."

THE END

THE COUNTRY LIFE PRESS
GARDEN CITY, N. Y.